ENTWINED PUBLISHING

About the Author

Megan Slayer, aka Wendi Zwaduk, is a multi-published, award-winning author of more than one-hundred short stories and novels. She's been writing since 2008 and published since 2009. Her stories range from the contemporary and paranormal to LGBTQ and BDSM themes. No matter what the length, her works are always hot, but with a lot of heart. She enjoys giving her characters a second chance at love, no matter what the form. She's been the runner up in the Kink Category at Love Romances Café as well as nominated at the LRC for best author, best contemporary, best ménage and best anthology. Her books have made it to the bestseller lists on Amazon.com.

When she's not writing, Megan spends time with her husband and son as well as three dogs and three cats. She enjoys art, music and racing, but football is her sport of choice.

Megan loves to hear from readers. You can find her contact information, website details and author profile page at https://www.firstforromance.com

COACHING LOVE

Dedication

To TPZ
To KC
To the Lucky Ducks

Daddy Needs a Date

COACHING LOVE

MEGAN SLAYER

ENTWINED PUBLISHING

Coaching Love
ISBN # 978-1-80250-289-3
©Copyright Megan Slayer 2025
Cover Art by Kelly Martin ©Copyright November 2025
Interior text design by Entwined Publishing
Published by Entice, an Entwined Publishing imprint

Published in 2025 by Entwined Publishing, United Kingdom.

Entwined Publishing is a division of Totally Entwined Group Limited.

Chapter One

"I'm tired of being alone." Bram Rode carried his briefcase to the ballfield, then up to the third row of the short bleachers. Watching his son's baseball practice would be so much more fun with someone to talk to.

He settled on the hard seat, one he'd grown accustomed to over the years, and observed the team at practice. Most of the players were in pairs in the outfield, tossing a ball between them, honing their skills at the game of catch.

Bram fiddled with the handle on his briefcase, but didn't open the latch. Something about the sweat, dirt and excitement of baseball — it'd never left him. Even after so many years away from playing the sport himself, he simply needed those sensations, and it was like he was right back in the midst of one of his own games.

He caught sight of the coach and his breath lodged in his throat. Alan Klane. If ever there was a man who could be considered walking temptation, it was Coach. Alan carried himself with an air of confidence — what coach didn't? But he was also muted. He didn't seem to argue with the umpires over bad calls or with the players for errors.

Alan stood near the fence, speaking to another parent. He'd never said anything about Bram being present at the practices, but with the players being in the seventh grade, they all needed a means of transportation to head home after. For Bram, it was easy—he followed his son over to the fields after school concluded and worked on his mountains of paperwork. He could keep an eye on his son while indulging in the game he loved.

"Are you still working on something?" Alan asked.

He glanced over at the coach, half-surprised Alan had spoken to him. He'd been lusting over Alan for the better part of two years. "Always."

Alan grinned. "Good to see you here."

"Gotta keep an eye on them." He flicked the tabs on his briefcase. Alan usually only spoke a few words to him, but when he did, the moment was never lost on Bram.

"They're coming along." Alan rested his elbows on the fence.

Alan might have been only a few yards away, but he felt a crackle. Bram shook his head. He had to be imagining things. It'd been so long since he'd flirted with someone. Was he even still any good at it?

The more he looked at Alan, the more he wanted to drool. He had strong, muscular corded arms. His smile brightened not only Bram's afternoon, but could light a small city. The warmth was infectious.

"You're always here watching," Alan said. "Kaysen's got a good arm."

"He does," he said. "Like yours." *Fuck.* He wasn't supposed to say that out loud.

Alan laughed. He shook his head and walked away.

Bram bit back his embarrassment. He'd said things that construed as crossing the line with his son's coach and now Alan had to think he was silly. But Alan did have nice arms. He'd bet Alan spent time in the batting cages at the sports complex he ran.

But so much for flirting. He massaged his forehead and plunked his briefcase on his lap. He should've known he'd be terrible at it. Chalk it up to being out of the dating pool for so long.

He pulled his tablet from his briefcase and fiddled with the sun guard, then read through his various emails. So many students in trouble, being referred to him, and not enough were getting notice for the academic prowess. He needed to change that climate at the school.

"Hey, Rode?"

He glanced up from the emails to see Alan at the fence again. Alan leaned on the chain link with one arm and crossed his ankles. He reminded Bram of a statue come to life.

If only he could have a chance with Alan. Maybe he'd find out what it was like to date a decent person. Christ, after his marriage that lasted way too long and ended in a colossal disaster, he wasn't sure he wanted to be with someone else. He could've been the entire reason the marriage fell apart.

"Rode? Rode-y? Hey, Rode!" Alan rattled the chain. "I wanted you to see your kid pitch."

Fuck. He was supposed to be paying attention, not getting lost in his thoughts about his ex.

Alan laughed. "Now will you look at me?" He grinned.

Alan's grin sent warmth through Bram's body. He bit back a groan and forced his gaze to Kaysen, his son.

Kaysen stood on the mound, a steely look in his eyes and the ball in his glove. He gave a slight nod, then shook his head, before winding up for the pitch. Bram admired his son's pitching form. He'd picked up a thing or two during their games of catch.

"He's got a good arm. Better than mine," Alan said. "He's got talent."

"He does." He watched his son throw the ball and pride swelled in his heart. Kaysen had been learning. When Kaysen pitched again, Bram watched him more like a scout, wanting to improve Kaysen's form. He could work with this, though. Kaysen had the talent, but needed refinement.

"Gonna have them run laps here in a moment for a cool down, then stretches." Alan remained by the fence. "You got here late."

He didn't think Alan had noticed. "Was in a meeting." There always seemed to be meetings.

"Yeah?" Alan turned his back on Bram, then spoke to the junior coach, Deion. Every few moments, he'd glance up at Bram and grin. It probably shouldn't please Bram that much to know he was being seen, but it did. He liked the notice. He smiled back. Was that crackle he'd felt earlier getting stronger? His flirting senses could be dull, but it sure appeared Alan's wink wasn't just positive coaching. After a few moments, Alan returned his focus to the players.

Bram resumed reading his emails, but kept one ear tuned to Alan, in case the conversation started up again. He enjoyed their chatting, even if it was near the end of practice.

He wasn't sure how much time had passed before he looked up again. Seemed like he spent too many precious minutes on email when he could've been watching his son. His kid was growing up too fast. All kids did.

He shook his head and darkened the tablet screen. He'd shortchanged Kaysen enough and made the decision. It was time to pay his son more attention. He looked up, but the team was busy running laps around the warning track.

So much for watching him pitch.

He packed up, then ambled down the stands to the fence. "Looked good today, Coach."

Alan finished speaking to Deion. "They did." He joined Bram at the chain link. "You've been here every practice this year and I thought you'd forgotten today. Good to see you're here."

"I don't like to miss it. It's time with my son." He placed the briefcase on the ground at his feet. "It's one of the few things we can bond over."

"Gotta have those things." Alan leaned on the fence and his arm brushed against Bram's. It was only a minor touch, and through the fabric of Bram's dress shirt, but the slight brush seared Bram to his core.

Bram bit back a groan. He hadn't been caressed by a lover or date or anyone in a remotely romantic way in so long. He had to stop thinking about Alan as dating material, but the possibility remained. "What do you have to have?"

It was a ridiculous question.

"What?" Alan asked. He inclined his head and grinned. "I'm sorry?"

"Never mind." He had to gather himself. "When I get nervous, I don't make much sense."

"That's not good for a principal, but I understand. It's not easy when you're flustered," Alan said. "You don't have to be with me."

The reassurance in Alan's words helped, but didn't take much of the embarrassment away. "I meant, you've got to have things that you bond over. Do you eat, sleep and breathe baseball?"

"No." Alan laughed again and patted Bram's arm. "I have enough of that over at the sports club. I like baseball and it's in my blood, but I'm not obsessed."

"Probably good. Keeps you objective." Dear God. *Keeps you objective?* He had to stop getting so involved in staff meetings and repeating the jargon. If this was how he flirted, it wasn't good.

Alan's smile grew in intensity. He patted Bram's arm again. "I know you're flustered, but it's okay. I know what you mean. It's nice to talk to someone about baseball, but it's also nice to step away from it for a while. Keeps you fresh."

"Yes." He would to get there eventually.

He noticed the glint in Alan's eyes and the crinkles at the corners. He had a dusting of hairs on his jaw, like he'd forgotten to shave, and his Adam's apple bobbed when he spoke. He had nice hands, too. Not gnarly from years of sports, but groomed, like he cared about his appearance. He didn't even seem to have any tattoos, not that Bram minded. Ink didn't bother him.

When he looked at Alan, an electric shock went through him. He wasn't sure he wanted to enter the dating pool yet. It'd been three years since his divorce, but the more he swept his gaze over Alan and the more he tried to awkwardly flirt, the more he considered giving dating a try. Maybe Alan would be interested.

It was worth the chance.

"I should go. I've got to round up the players and get them packed up to end practice," Alan said. "I'll see you at the next one?"

"Always." He hated to miss them.

"Good. I like involved parents who give me space to do my job, but are invested in their kids," Alan said. "Glad you're at the school, too. You have a positive influence on the students."

"Thanks." This time, he touched Alan's arm and swore his body tingled. He suppressed a whimper. "See you at the next practice?"

"You will. I never seem to leave here." Alan grinned, then winked again and lingered another moment before walking away.

He stayed by the fence, almost disbelieving the moment had transpired between him and Alan. All the times he'd ogled him, he'd finally seen him and liked what he'd observed. Now that he'd had more of a chat with him beyond the simple greetings, he enjoyed Alan's ability to put him at ease and fluster him at the same time. He'd love to have another conversation with him. Might even like to spend time with Alan outside of a team practice session.

If he wanted that to be possible, he'd have to make it happen.

Would someone question him? It probably didn't look good for the coach and the principal to be involved, especially with Kaysen on the team. He preferred to conduct himself above reproach, but he was drawn to Alan.

Maybe Alan was just being nice and wasn't drawn to him in return. Maybe the crackle was all in his head. That was a distinct possibility.

But Alan had given him hope. He wasn't great at flirting, but not terrible, either. If he started putting himself out there and gave dating a try, he just might find the guy to share forever with. It might take a while. Not every man out there was looking for a long-term relationship. Alan might not want one.

Alan might not even be gay.

That settled it—he'd dip his toe into the dating pool. Not jump headlong into the deep end. He had a tendency to jump before he thought and hope the outcome would work, but this was too important to move too quickly.

Yes, he'd take his time and find the right person. Take a few chances. Go out on more than one date and see what happened. Even if he got his heart broken, it was time to give love another try.

* * * *

"I've decided to enter the dating pool," Bram said, leaning back in his seat. He'd been mulling this over for the last two days. "I'm tired of being alone." He adjusted the phone against his ear. Normally, he left the annoying device on speaker on his desk, but this was a private conversation and the walls tended to have ears.

"You're ready? Are you sure?" Dante Collins asked. "Did you discuss this with the others or declare it on your own?"

Bram rubbed his forehead. He loved his college friends like they were his brothers. They'd gone through four years and so many events together all while becoming a tight unit. They guys were each other's lifeline. They were his support group and he couldn't imagine not having their input. "I need to set up a group chat."

"Why don't you do this as a video meeting?" Dante asked. "Then we can all join in. Plus, it's better when you can see the other person's face."

"I could." He probably should. "Just not tonight. I've got to get Kaysen to baseball practice and still have paperwork. We've got five teachers out tomorrow due to meetings and I need subs."

"You could do that later. Chat during practice," Dante said. "Tim and Josef will have thoughts."

"On how to schedule the right subs for the right classrooms?" He knew what Dante meant, but he liked to deflect when it came to his love life. He'd opened the door to this, but part of him wished he'd kept his mouth shut.

"Bram."

"I know."

"Why are you hesitant? You're lonely, and I'm sure Kaysen would like another guy in your life. I bet there's someone out there — that isn't Gil — who would treat you both well."

"I'm sure." The mention of Gil's name stung. His ex-husband had left them three years ago and the hurt was still strong.

"Gil wasn't kind at the end," Dante said. "Yeah, we all thought he was decent enough people when you first started seeing him and thought he might shape up once you were together a while. Hell, I even thought he'd get his head out of his ass once you adopted Kay, but he never grew up and you were the only one who adopted your son."

"I know."

"Time changed him, but that wasn't just that. He already had that terrible streak in him."

"I know that, too." Lots of things had changed about Gil, but mostly his ex had decided he needed to be free. The Gil from twenty-five years ago was one man and the current day one was a different version.

"He might have changed, but so did you. You know who you are now, and you're a good dad. You're a great principal. Don't sell yourself short because of Gil."

"I'm not." Not out loud. He could do more with Kaysen to make his son a better young man. As for his job, he spent too much time at the school, but he wanted to do the best for the students. Some days it seemed like no matter what he did, it wasn't enough for everyone. "What if I don't find someone? What if I do the guys don't want a kid?"

"Then they aren't right for you."

That was so right, but damn. "I'll try to get a video chat going while Kay's at practice. We'll be at the ballfields, okay? The service might not be the best."

"It'll be fine. I'm texting Josef and Tim right now," Dante said. "Don't sell yourself short and don't give up. There's someone out there for you. Gil was part of your life, but he's not all of it. You have a second act and it's time you take the stage. The right person is out there and you should definitely try dating. You might enjoy it."

"Sure." He sighed as Kaysen walked into his office. "I need to go. It's time for practice."

"Sure. I'll talk to you in a while."

"Yeah." He hung up and rolled right up to his desk. "How was tutoring?"

Kayson shrugged. "Gavin gets it, but he doesn't want to do the work and Trent is giving up. They're feeding off each other. They're in third grade and giving up. How?"

"They need the right motivation, but you're doing the right things."

"Sure." Kayson plopped onto the chair. "Coach Klane said I'm getting better at my pitches. He visited gym class today to recruit the elementary teams and pointed me out to the younger kids."

"Good." He tucked his paperwork into his case. "I'm proud of you."

"He wants to move me from relief pitching to starting."

"I'm glad." He'd seen that when he'd practiced with Kaysen. "I knew you had talent and I'm glad he's fostering that."

"Gil always told me I was terrible."

He winced again at the mention of Gil's name. His ex-husband had been rough on Kaysen, despite never actually adopting him. "He was jealous of your talent." He'd never told Kaysen that before, but it was the truth.

"He was?"

"He was." He zipped the case shut. "Get a drink from the fridge so you're hydrated. Did you get a granola bar?"

"I had one, and a fruit bar," Kaysen said. He left his chair to retrieve the bottle from the small fridge. "Why was he jealous? He was a ballplayer."

"Let's go to the car." He picked up his belongings and nodded to the door.

"Are you dodging?"

His son was too smart. "No, I'm waiting until we have privacy."

"Dad?"

"It's nothing terrible." He left his desk and ushered his son out of the room. He locked the door behind them, then went into the exterior offices. One of the janitors waved.

"See you tomorrow, Rich. Have a good night." He followed Kaysen to the car.

"Is Gil coming back?" Kaysen asked.

He hated that Kaysen called Gil by his first name, but after the split, Gil had lost the right to be called anything else. He wasn't a dad to Kaysen. "No, he's not."

"Good. I hate pitching when he watches." Kaysen tossed his bookbag into the trunk.

He'd bet Kaysen did hate when Gil watched. Gil could be punishing with his critiques. Gil might have been a ballplayer, but he'd never had Kaysen's natural talent.

He joined Kaysen in the car. Once the door had shut, he exhaled. He had few secrets, but he wanted this conversation to be private.

"So?" Kaysen asked. "Why was he jealous?"

"Gil played ball in college."

"That's how you met him, duh."

"It is, but I was on the baseball team and he was part of the pick-up league for those who weren't quite ready for the varsity team."

"He couldn't make the practices?"

"He wasn't good enough to make the team. He tried out every year and was cut. He hated that I had a spot on the team all four years and he didn't. I thought he was fine and had gotten past the perceived slight. I was so young and trusting when he said he'd gotten over it."

"He hadn't?"

"No." He engaged the engine. "He harbored it all those years. It was there the whole time, but I tried not to see it. When you showed natural talent like mine, the jealousy came back."

Kaysen snorted. "What a jerk."

"He could be."

"I'm a kid. He's an adult. He should get over it— that's what he would've told me."

"It is." Things with Gil had been much more complicated, but he'd kept that to himself. Kaysen

18

needed to know some of those reasons and explanations, but they weren't everything. He drove away from the school to the parks behind the school campus.

"I'm glad he's not coming back. I want to play for the varsity team," Kaysen said. "If I keep practicing, I might be able to. Coach Klane says I've got the talent."

"You do." Coach Klane was pretty smart. "I'll get you to practice."

Chapter Two

"Are you going to try dating again?" Kaysen asked. "You seem lonely."

"You heard my call, didn't you?" He'd expected Kaysen would eavesdrop.

"I couldn't help it. You were talking so loud. Tell Uncle Dante I said hi."

Kaysen had a point, and he'd find out eventually. Plus, he liked that Kaysen had resumed calling Dante his uncle. Dante, Tim and Josef were the most family they had.

"Are you?"

"Yes. I'm dipping a toe into the waters, so don't think I've found someone or I'm going all-in." He pulled into the parking lot and headed for the shaded area to the south of the fences.

Kaysen laughed. "Are you scared?"

"Why are you laughing? It's not funny."

"It's not funny at all, but the guys have asked me when you're going to date."

"The guys?"

"The team."

Good God. He didn't want to be part of the teenage rumor mill. "Why do they care?" he asked and pulled into the first free spot, backing into the space along the fence.

"Because Brian and Everlee's mom wants to set you up with her friend Alice and I told them you weren't interested. Their mother said you'd change your mind when she was done with you."

Done with him? Like he was a project. "They do know I'm gay?" He'd come to Lakewood with Gil and never hid his marriage.

"Everyone does."

"And they're both convinced they can what...save me?"

"I guess so," Kaysen replied. "It's silly. You're not going to change because she wants you to. You have to be yourself."

He couldn't have said it better himself.

"You're not going to let their mom find you a date, are you?"

"No."

"She wants to say you're her best client. Why do adults do that?"

"Oh, so Natasha is a matchmaker?" He should've known. "What do you mean?" He switched off the engine and opened the car windows.

"They push in where they're not wanted."

"Well, she can think she's helping, but she's not. I don't need a matchmaker, and the uncles wouldn't let me anyway." He wasn't even sure he should be dating at all. "What do you think?" They had about ten minutes until practice started and only a couple of the players were there already.

"About?"

"My dating — anyone. It's been a while since Gil left and it's been just you and me at the house. How do you feel about me looking?" He needed to involve his son. What affected his life affected Kaysen's life too.

"Dad, you're lonely and you deserve someone. I hope you find someone and that it works out. Just don't take Gil back."

"Why would I do that?" he asked. He had no desire to have his ex in his life again.

"Because he's texted me saying he misses us and wishes I'd tell you that."

"Block him." His anger flared. His ex shouldn't be contacting Kaysen this way. Gil hadn't wanted to adopt Kaysen. He hadn't signed any of the paperwork, despite agreeing to Bram adopting Kaysen, leaving himself legally unobligated. Once Bram had brought Kaysen home, Gil kept the boy at arm's length. Now he wanted some sort of involvement? Wanted to put Kaysen in the middle? *No way.*

"I did. He tried to contact me on social media and I blocked him there, too." Kaysen shrugged. "I want you to be happy, but I don't think Gil would make you that way."

"For being thirteen, you're very wise."

"I learned from you, Dad." Kaysen grinned. "I see Coach Klane. Better go."

"I'll be here."

"Paperwork?"

"Always, but I also want to talk to the support group."

"Tell the uncles I said hi." Kaysen left the car. He collected his baseball gear from the trunk before waving and rushing away.

He sagged in the car seat and rubbed his eyes. He didn't need that much help finding a date, did he?

He shook his head, then picked up his phone and tapped the icon to open a video chat with Dante, Tim and Josef. Tim answered first.

"Hi. You look stressed. Is it that hard to find a date?" Tim asked. "Sucks to be you."

"I knew you'd be a smart ass about this." He should be annoyed with Tim, but his friend didn't mean anything bad. "I haven't even started looking."

"I knew you hadn't. You're cautious," Tim said. "You got hurt bad, too."

"I did. Maybe I shouldn't bother." He wasn't sure.

"No. If you think it might be time, then you need to try. You can't be alone forever," Tim said.

Dante entered the chat. "Did you talk him into doing it yet?"

"You've discussed me." Bram sighed. "Geez."

"We might have," Tim said. "We worry about you."

"Why?" He was just fine.

"You're lonely, and we've seen you retract into yourself over the last two years," Dante said.

"I have not." Maybe he had.

"Who do you have in mind?" Tim asked.

"I haven't thought about it," Bram said. "Truth."

"You're fibbing," Dante said. "Where's Josef?"

"He's trying to leave work," Tim replied. "You have a type, Bram. You like sporty types."

"So?" He did. "I like dark-haired men, too."

"You do," Tim said. "Are you using an app? Do you need a wingman? Or maybe for us to look over your profile?"

"God." He didn't want to be on a dating app.

"Matchmaker?" Dante asked. "We could try one of those."

"I'm not interested." He'd go the more traditional route. "I'll try the clubs."

"And successfully pick up someone?" Tim asked. "You're too shy."

"I'm intervening," Dante said. "No question."

"Dante." He wasn't a child.

"You're a principal. You can't just go to a club. You have to be smart about this, and remember your image," Tim said. "We won't let you get embarrassed."

"I agree," Dante said. "You need to think of who might see you. Where is Josef? If he was here, he'd agree. Wonder if he got stuck in traffic?"

It was useless to argue. "Then what do I do?" he asked. "You can all tell I'm tired of being alone and tired of going to bed by myself while staring at the same four walls. My heart still hurts because of what Gil did. I never thought he'd do that. I thought we had what it took to go the distance. I thought we'd have forever and he walked away." It wasn't like him to let his emotions get the best of him, but when they did, he couldn't rein them in right away.

"Did you, though?" Tim asked. "He didn't want anything to do with Kaysen."

"He hated that Kaysen was good at sports," Dante said. "And he got jealous that you were athletic. He wasn't good at hiding that, or his disdain for us. He thought we were intruding."

He wasn't sure what to say and hated to be so defeated.

"He argued with you a lot," Tim said. "How many times did you have to reschedule or miss stuff we did because of him? We lost out on a lot of time together because he wasn't about to be upstaged or bothered by us."

"He forbade you from meeting up with us," Dante said.

"I'm sorry." He had no other words.

"Why are you sorry?" Josef asked. "I missed a bunch. I should be sorry. Work got crazy, then I got stuck behind a cement truck."

"It's fine." He could only take a little more reminding. His heart ached. "I was foolish."

"No, you weren't," Dante said. "You were in love."

"And he wasn't," Tim said. "Gil was an ass. He brought you down, but you liked him and you don't have to apologize."

"Are you going to date again?" Josef asked. "You so should."

"Thanks." So much for his excitement to enter the dating pool. "I'm making a mistake."

"You are not," Josef said. "You're doing what you always do. You're backing down because you're being kind. You're trying to make everyone happy and you're trying too hard. You want everyone to be included and no one to get hurt. You don't have to do that—life is messy and hard. People do get hurt. Gil should be left in the past so you can have a future."

"You're... I don't know what." Bram groaned. Josef was right. He tended to look at his ex through a different lens than everyone else. He'd given Gil too much of a pass.

"You need to try someone better," Dante said. "Who's that guy behind you? I can barely see him through the back window, but he's cute."

Guy behind him? He glanced over his shoulder and noticed Kaysen with the coach. "That's Kay's coach. If he's coming over, I need to go."

"He's cute. Ever consider him?" Josef asked and laughed. "But it would help to know if he's gay and interested first."

He wished he saw their humor. "I'm not just walking up to someone to ask if they're interested and if they're gay." For all he knew, Coach Klane wasn't.

"Okay, so where are you looking and how are you going about it?" Dante asked. "Answer quick."

"No." He loved Dante and the rest of the support group, but they could be a hindrance at times. "I'll figure it out."

"No, you won't. You'll get nervous and quit early," Tim said. "You stumbled into the relationship with the ass."

Bluntly put, but true. He'd been targeted by Gil. As for quitting, he disagreed. "Then who do you suggest?"

"A wingman, or at least visit a club where you won't get shit for being there," Tim said. "Trust me."

He supposed Tim was right. He stared at the four windows open on his phone. He should've used his tablet for this, but he noticed how different the four of them were, yet they looked out of each other. He should trust them. "I'll try the Rainbow. They've got an open mic night."

"Don't do comedy," Dante said. "No one gets your comedy."

"I know, but I figured the guys would be more honest because they're getting the chance to perform." He spied Kaysen coming back toward the car. Either he'd been hurt at practice or there was a problem. "I need to go and be a parent."

"Go. Kaysen deserves your attention," Tim said and closed his window.

Josef winked. "Call me if you need me." He ended his chat link, leaving Bram alone with Dante.

"You should be happy and should be loved for who you are," Dante said. "Don't settle. Take your time and find this mystery guy — whoever he is — and if you need me or the other guys, just say something."

"Thanks." He closed the chat and abandoned his phone on the console before leaving the car. He joined Kaysen and Coach Klane along the fence just behind the car. "What do you know?"

"Dad! I'm starting the game tomorrow and on Saturday," Kaysen said, practically vibrating. "You said I had it in me and I do."

"You do." He hugged Kaysen. Pride welled in him. He'd known Kaysen had the talent. He'd never been much of a pitcher himself — more of an outfielder — yet he knew his son had something special about him. "Good job."

"May I have a word with you?" Coach Klane asked. "We need to talk."

"Sure." He let go of Kaysen. "Do you need to get back to practice?"

"Yeah. I asked Coach if I could tell you, but we still have forty-five minutes." Kaysen beamed, then ran back to the field.

He wouldn't lie — he was a bit choked up. Yes, it was a game, but still, his son had done something. He turned his attention to the coach. "I'm sorry. You wanted a word?"

"I do."

"Something wrong?" He might as well be blunt. "His grades are fine. Just checked them."

"His status isn't in question," Coach Klane said. "Call me Alan. No, I wanted to be sure you were okay with him pitching as a starter. Some parents aren't."

"You can call me Bram. Yeah, I played ball when I was his age through college. I know what it takes and it's fine. If he's got talent, use it. Foster it." He'd keep an eye on Kaysen, but he'd also give him the freedom to play the game.

"You played? What position?" Allan asked. "How did I not know?"

"I don't advertise," Bram said. "I was a first baseman, then right field. I played through college, but didn't bother to go out for the draft. I didn't have the dedication. I wanted to teach instead."

"What'd you teach?"

"History." He usually didn't discuss this, but the words tumbled out. "Then I got the chance to become a vice principal and jumped." He wasn't about to say that his choice involved needing a pay increase to support Gil. That wasn't anyone's business.

"Very cool. I quit teaching to run the gym and batting cages. It paid better and kept me in the game, plus involved a lot less stress," Alan said.

"Good. You should do what you love." Why'd he say it that way? He sounded like a motivational poster.

"Well, as long as you're okay with him pitching, he'll start tomorrow's game and the one on Saturday. It's not guaranteed that he's staying in the rotation, but he deserves the chance to prove himself this way."

"He does, and I approve," Bram said. It was so odd. He'd never had to have conversations like this with the other coaches. "Anything else?"

Alan hesitated. "Are you interested in running the concession stand on Saturday?"

"Was that the real reason you asked?" He'd been conned into volunteering plenty of times.

"Yes and no."

He shook his head. He didn't have much else to do and he'd be able to watch Kaysen pitch. "Sure. What's the no?"

"I wanted to get some help for the stand, but I also just wanted to speak to you. I never really get the chance to talk to the parents."

"Understandable."

"I'll email you with the times." Alan hesitated again, then waved and walked away.

The pause annoyed him because it felt like there was something else to say. But then again, Alan might have been thinking about something else. Or maybe that crackle in the air wasn't all in Bram's mind.

Bram sighed and returned to his car. He needed to find a partner for some bedroom time and relax before he started believing things were more than they were. He needed companionship and love, but he'd let that go for now.

He watched Alan walk away. Alan had a nice ass—just enough to grab and with a slight wiggle.

Except Alan might not be gay.

Oh well.

To the dating pool!

Chapter Three

Alan glanced over his shoulder and wished he'd had just a little more courage. He'd had an eye on Bram for a long time now. The man was too beautiful. It wasn't fair that Bram could be so handsome and athletic. He was too good to be true.

He'd heard Bram was single. No word on if he was interested in dating, but if so, Alan wanted a chance.

"Coach?" Caleb Whitcomb strode up to him. "I heard you've demoted my son to the bullpen."

"It's not a demotion." He'd expected this. Most parents had thoughts on what their child could do and where the child should play. Many parents overestimated their player's ability. A few were more pragmatic, but not many.

Caleb thought his son was the best on the team.

"It's a demotion. He's a starter. A star. Only the starters are seen by the scouts," Caleb said. "How will Dino be noticed if he's not a starter?"

"Practicing. Get him to do some extra reps and he'll be fine. He's getting complacent in his pitching." It wasn't the answer the parent wanted, but it was the truth.

"Complacent!" Caleb shouted. "How dare you?"

"I'm the coach. I see his talent and it could be cultivated more, but if he's getting complacent because he's resting on his talents alone, then he won't progress. Ask any professional athlete and they'll tell you the same thing. You always have to be learning and honing your skills. I'm doing my part, but it's up to all of us. Encourage him to ice his arm more, too. Have a game of catch with him to keep it loose. I'm working on his technique. He's throwing too much side arm."

"You're lying."

"Okay, then I'm lying." He wasn't arguing any longer. "I need to get back to the boys. Excuse me." He left Caleb by the dugout and strode to the outfield. The players gathered around him, chattering and laughing.

"What're we doing, Coach?" George, one of the outfielders, asked.

"I want you to do ten laps, running the bases, then pair up for a game of catch in the outfield. I want to be sure we're ready. Everyone on the team, currently playing or not, are talented. We all need to keep practicing, no matter how long we've been playing. A few rounds of catch will do us good. Toss until you miss, then switch with the pair next to you. I'll jump in here and there to join you."

"You're gonna run more laps?" Jimmy asked. "I saw you running this morning."

"Never hurts to be in shape." He clapped his hands. "Go. I'm watching."

His assistant coach, Deion, rushed up to him. "Whitcomb is persistent."

"That's why I walked. I can only put up with him for so long. They all know better and only a very few have the talent to do our job. It's not as easy as it looks. He'd struggle if he had to put up with twenty newly minted teens all filled with testosterone and excitement."

"He would." Deion folded his arms. "I saw you talking to Mr. Rode. Finally got up the nerve to speak to him?"

"And it was difficult as hell," he confessed out of the earshot of the players. He'd admitted to Deion that he had a crush on Bram Rode. He'd worried if someone knew he was attracted to Bram, they'd question why Kaysen was on the team. Kaysen had talent and had earned his spot with the Panthers fairly.

"But you did talk to him and that's good. You need to do something," Deion said. "If you don't find someone or get some, you're going to explode."

"Shut up." Deion was right, though. "I might." He'd lusted after Bram for the last year. Every time he thought he'd get the courage to talk to Bram, he lost it.

"So what'd you manufacture as the reason to chat with him?" Deion asked. "I saw you go over there with a purpose."

"I moved Kaysen to a starter. He got excited and wanted to tell his dad, so I followed. I said I needed permission."

"No, you don't."

"I know that."

"You sly dog. You got him to talk to you."

"I did."

"And? Did you feel a spark?" Deion nodded. "You did."

"I did."

"And you asked him out?"

"No." He nodded as the players hustled to the outfield. "We should join them."

"We should, but you didn't take your swing. You need to try. Maybe it won't work, but never let it pass without an attempt."

"I know." He wanted to try again after splitting from Rae. He'd stayed single for far too long. But he'd sworn Rae was so terrible because he wasn't worthy of being loved. He still didn't think he deserved it.

"So why'd you chicken out? I knew you did. You do that every time to sabotage yourself. Because of Rae? He's history and he's also terrible. You never should've stuck with him as long as you did."

"Deion."

"I'm serious."

"I know." He said that too much. He picked up a spare baseball. He should join the team. "I chickened out because he's a principal and I run a fitness club."

"You're a coach. He's a principal. It's cute, and how fantasies start."

"Deion," he said. His assistant coach needed to stop. Not only could the team possibly hear them, but Deion had encouraged thoughts Alan didn't deserve. He shouldn't imagine such things.

"Stop. You'll sabotage yourself to the point of being alone again. I'm sorry, but no. You're not doing it, even if I have to push."

"You don't have to do that."

"I do and I will. You're a good man who needs to be treated like a king. He might be able to do that." Deion tossed a glove at him. "So was he happy that Kaysen's going to pitch?"

"Yes." He remained at the edge of the outfield, just out of earshot of the players. "I also asked him if he'd help on Saturday in the concession stand."

"And he agreed?"

"He did."

"You'll call him with the details?"

"Said I'd email him."

"Alan."

"What?"

"You should call him."

"I will, but I don't want to rush this." He groaned. "I can't jump right in and demand a date or anything else with him because he's possibly not interested. If I push, he might walk away and I don't want to screw this up before it's started."

"You won't chicken out again?"

He sighed. "No, but I won't rush it, either. There's nothing wrong with going slower. I like to use the pace of the game to my advantage."

"Unless you're allowing yourself to be a human rain delay."

"Ouch." He appreciated Deion's sense of humor. "I'll try to talk to him on Saturday. We have a break and the Whitcombs are having a team bonding thing during the downtime."

"I know. I was invited."

"I wasn't." But he liked that Deion would be there to observe.

"You're the coach. I assumed you were."

"Caleb Whitcomb thinks he can do better, so I'm giving him the chance to try. It's not as easy as it looks." He fitted the glove on his hand and nodded. "Report back to me so I know how to handle the situation for game two. I trust you."

"I got your back. This is our team and we've worked too hard with these young men to give up now. Besides, if we keep playing at this level, we're nearly certain to have the third seed in the tournament. I don't want to risk that."

"Agreed, which is why I'm not stopping Whitcomb, but I'm crawling right in afterward to handle it when things blow up."

"Good." Deion slapped the ball in his glove. "Now do the same thing with your dating situation—when it happens, make the catch."

"More sports jokes?"

Deion shrugged. "You knew what I meant."

"I do."

"So do it. Give yourself a chance and make a move. We have three games this week and we're poised for the playoffs. If we keep going in the tournament, you might have lots of time to talk to him."

He knew who *him* was. "Okay." He wasn't about to argue. "Go out there so we can model for them. They need to see us participating."

"We always do." Deion hustled away from him.

Time to play ball. He shouldn't be worried about his past or dating or anything else. The team needed him and he should be coaching.

* * * *

Alan concluded practice and waited for the parents to pick up their players. He refused to leave until everyone was with their parent or ride. Hell, he wasn't permitted to leave unless everyone was gone. He'd sent Deion home early to pick up his son at daycare.

Caleb Whitcomb stopped Alan. "Coach, I have the games for the team-building situation on Saturday. Mr. McLaren said he's joining in, if you don't mind losing him in the concession stand."

"It's fine. I'm hoping the team enjoys what you've got planned. Just make sure no one gets injured before the game. We need everyone healthy for our run for the championship."

Caleb nodded, then grinned. "So Dino could pitch in the playoffs?"

"Yes." He'd probably have to.

"Great. Have a good night." Caleb walked away, leaving him by the dugout.

One day he'd figure parents out. Then again, once he did, he'd get out of coaching. He refused to coach the game to please the parents.

The players had to love the game. That's what mattered.

He noticed Bram and Kaysen at the fence. If he was going to talk to Bram and keep it natural, then this was his chance. "Everything okay?"

"Yeah." Bram blushed. "Kaysen thought he lost his glove."

"You did?" It wasn't unheard of for a player to lose a piece of equipment, but he knew Kaysen had his glove. "Did you check the bat bags?"

Kaysen shook his head, then jogged over to the massive containers.

"Kids," Bram said. "They'd forget their head if it wasn't attached."

"Nah. He's got a lot on his mind. Pitching is huge," Alan said. "So while he's looking, I'll explain Saturday."

"Yes."

"I'd help him, but I believe in letting them struggle and look on their own before helping. That lets them be a little more independent," Alan said. "The glove might be in there or in his own bag. I saw his hitting gloves, though, so I tucked those in the bag. He might be looking for them. Don't want them to get stolen."

"Smart. We're lucky to have you as a coach. You're good for the players," Bram said. "You've managed to do wonders for Kay's self-esteem."

"I want to build my players up," he replied. "And Kaysen's got the talent. He's a good pitcher. I want him to keep working on controlling his pitches better, but he's on the right track."

"Good." Bram folded his arms. "I'd think he's found that glove, but looks like Nicki just found him."

Nicki? He glanced over his shoulder. "Oh, Justin's sister. Yeah, she's sweet on him."

"Sweet on?" Bram laughed. "I haven't heard that in so long. I try to use that kind of wording at school because my students are so young and don't need to grow up that fast."

"I agree." He chuckled and matched Bram's stance. "I try to keep my language G-rated so the kids have a good influence and example."

"Smart. I wish more would do that. It's a good thing for the kids to have good models," Bram said. "I see so many influences that aren't."

"And that's why I do what I do." He faced Bram. "So, on Saturday…" He'd gotten himself sidetracked.

"Good call giving them another moment. She's been chasing him for a year, but they're thirteen," Bram said. "I'm sorry. Ever since my divorce, I haven't been too interested in trying to find someone and it makes me nauseous to see anyone in love. Terrible, isn't it? People should be happy."

"It's hard when you've been hurt." He really should be discussing the concession stand situation, but he was learning so much about Bram. He liked this conversation. Maybe he was imagining things, but they did have a spark. "Are you okay?"

"No, but I hide it well. Kaysen doesn't need to know." Bram bowed his head. "I don't normally talk about that stuff."

"The past? It's okay. You needed to get it out."

"I don't open up, you know? I want people to see this image of me that's got everything together. Disciplined. If they know I'm miserable or my love life is yuck and I'm depressed, then they'll wonder about my abilities at school."

"You might be right, or you might be reading too much into it. They want to know you're human, too. Don't forget that."

"True." Bram met his gaze. "You're a good coach."

"Thanks. I haven't done anything."

"You have and don't realize it," Bram said. "You've got me considering, not just talking about, getting back out there, but actually doing it. I shouldn't have to hide, you're right."

Well, what a huge form of praise he hadn't earned. "So what are you going to do?"

"I talked to the support group and they want me to go forward."

"Support group? For what? Divorcees?" He didn't need one for being divorced, but he could use the support if it had to do with broken relationships.

"Oh, it's my friend group from college. We all lived together in a four-person dorm suite then apartment off campus to save money and became close. Each of us took a different path in life, but we're all gay and, in our own fashion, struggling, so we lean on each other."

"Then it's a good thing you have them. You're stronger than you think, though." That sounded so bland, but whatever. He meant it.

"I am, but I'm also scared."

He wanted to ask *of what*, but didn't. "Did you all date each other?"

"No, oddly enough. That might be why we're all still friends. No one tried to jump in bed with anyone else." Bram laughed. "I'll introduce you sometime."

"Thanks. I could use some support."

"What's wrong?"

"Just inching into the dating pool like you are." It was hard to admit that. *Damn.*

"Rough ex?"

"You could say that." He wasn't ready to discuss Rae yet.

"I hear you. Everyone saw the public and messy split I went through and that's why I'm hesitant. I don't want everyone to look at it with a microscope." Bram cleared his throat. "So about Saturday." He lowered his voice. "Kaysen's on the way."

"Understood." He switched his tone. "So Saturday, we need you to meet the stand manager, Shelley, at two. She'll have you working within five minutes and your shift is until four or four-thirty. I'll be in around two-thirty to help."

"Why? You're a coach."

"The team is doing something without me and I didn't have a coaches meeting then. I might as well help," Alan said. "It's good to give back." He might also get the chance to talk to Bram more.

"Nice. The team should include you, though."

"I have Deion spying for me."

"Good." Bram nodded once. "I'll be there. Might even show up a little early so I know what I'm doing. The first game should be over by one-thirty. I'll feed Kaysen and jump in."

"Cool. I look forward to it." He should've said we. Had Bram caught on to his slip? He hoped not.

"So do I." Bram held out his hand. "Find it?"

Kaysen sighed. "I did. I found Nicki, too. She wants to go together."

"And?" Bram asked.

Alan kept quiet, but he sort of wanted to know, too.

"I told her I wanted to be friends. I'm a kid. I don't need a girlfriend," Kaysen said. "Buddy said I need to go out with her so I'm not a wuss or sus. I'm not. I just don't want to date anyone yet."

"There's nothing wrong with that," Alan said. "You be you. That's what's important."

"I agree with Coach. When you're ready, you'll know." Bram grinned and took the gloves from Kaysen. "I didn't date until I was seventeen."

"And you were confused until you were seventeen," Kaysen said. "I know. You've told me."

"I guess I've gotten to be a broken record," Bram said.

"You glitched, Dad," Kaysen corrected. "Let's go."

"I'm embarrassing you?" Bram asked and winked.

"Yes." Kaysen hurried to the car and climbed into the vehicle, hiding on the front seat.

Bram continued to laugh. "I shouldn't give him so much trouble, but I love to keep him humble. Plus, I sleep better when he's annoyed. It's a dad thing."

Alan wasn't sure what to do. He wanted to swat Bram on the shoulder. Before he realized what he was doing, he clapped Bram right on the biceps.

"Gonna tell me *good game*?" Bram asked, but didn't pull away.

"Yes," he replied. He moved his hand, but not before sparks shot through his body. Electricity seemed to zap his fingertips. From Bram? Sure felt that way. "Good game."

Bram laughed again and the warm sound enveloped Alan like a coat. He never wanted to get rid of the good feeling. He missed this kind of electricity. Did Bram feel it, too?

He wasn't sure.

"See you tomorrow at practice," Bram said, then walked away.

"See you." He loved that Bram got so involved with his son's life. Many parents didn't.

He'd always wondered what it'd be like to be a parent, but his teaching career and baseball interfered with that. He'd missed his chance.

Not that Rae had wanted kids.

Rae saw children as hindrances. They weren't, but he'd never get Rae to change his mind.

Rae always knew best.

At least he believed he did.

Alan picked up the remains of the practice equipment and Sal, one of the high school coaches, strode onto the field. "Saw you out here. Are you good? I heard your team is headed for the playoffs."

"They are." He bagged the last bat he'd missed, then zipped the bag shut. "They've got promise and I'm sure you'll be happy when they make their way up to the high school."

"I hope so. I've got a bunch of juniors and seniors. My younger players have a long way to go to develop," Sal said. "I saw Rode here."

"His son is one of the better prospects. I'm going to start him Saturday on the mound. I'd like him to develop more, but he'll be good once he gains a little confidence."

"Sweet." Sal rested his hands on his hips. "You know Rode was a ballplayer?"

"I did. Why?"

"His kid gets it honest."

"His son was adopted—but he seems to have gleaned his father's talent." He picked up the two left-handed gloves and put them in the front pouch of the bag. "I got him to helm the concession stand on Saturday."

"Perfect. I've been trying to get his help. It looks good when the admin helps. Like we're all on the same team."

"We are." He shrugged, then collected the last of the balls. He carried the three bags of equipment to the shed. "I wanted him to help and he is."

"Yeah." Sal followed him. "I hear it's about time he started dating."

"Huh?" He wasn't fond of discussing other people's love lives. Yes, he hoped Bram was indeed ready to date, but he wasn't pushing. It wasn't his place.

"He's looking for love. One of the moms heard from the parking lot where he was talking about it. I heard her say he needed dick."

That didn't sound right. "Could be a rumor and not true."

"Maybe, but it was a big deal three years ago when he split from his husband. He might be looking for dick. It's possible."

"It is, but it's also possible that it's a rumor cooked up to make someone look good for knowing some inside information." He closed the supply shed door. "Doesn't matter. It's not my business and I won't pry."

"It should be."

"Why?"

"You'd be good for him."

"I don't know." *Someone else has noticed? Holy hell.*

"You do. Think about it. You're single. He's single. You're fun and so is he. People want you to get together." Sal winked, then walked away without another word.

Good God. Now he was the subject of rumors. He hated that kind of attention. He wanted that for his ability to play baseball and his dedication to the community, not his dating life.

Not that he hadn't considered asking Bram out. He had. Only like one thousand times. But it didn't look good. Bram's son was on his team. It might considered a conflict. But that didn't make Bram any less appealing.

He couldn't deny his attraction. He'd always been a sucker for men in nice clothes. Men who knew how to be commanding.

That's what had gotten him into trouble before. He'd dated the coach of another team and that caused him problems. They weren't even in the same league, but it hadn't mattered.

It looked bad.

Might look bad with Bram, too.

Deion wanted him to call Bram. Sal thought they'd be good together. The rumor mill wanted them together. He'd thought he and Rae were good and he'd been wrong. He could be wrong about Bram.

He shook his head and closed the gate to the field. He needed to stop second-guessing himself and try. Slow and steady wasn't bad.

Right?

He might even find Mr. Right.

He sighed.

Might.

Chapter Four

Bram picked up the last of his go-bag and checked his watch. "Kay? We need to go." He'd be early for the pre-game warm-ups like Kaysen wanted. His internal watch pushed him to keep going because he hated being late — even if he was early.

Of all the things in life, being late drove him the craziest. Why run behind when one could get there on time or early and prevent issues?

It made perfect sense to him.

But he wasn't thirteen, either. He'd never understand the thirteen-year-old mind. Not really.

"Kay? Are you ready?"

Kaysen rushed down the stairs. "Pre-game nerves." He blushed. "Sorry."

"That's okay. This is why we run ahead of schedule. If something like that happens, then we've got a cushion. It's fine. Are you okay?" He hated repeating the word, but he tended to babble when he worried.

Kaysen could have a tummy ache, could have stomach flu…could just be nervous.

He had to stop overthinking.

"I'm fine. I'm worried about the game. What if I screw up? What if I flame out?" Kaysen asked. "Thursday I pitched well, but today… I'm scared." He groaned.

"You don't think I wasn't worried before my games? It's natural. When you stop being scared and get cocky, now that's when you've got a problem. You're going to be fine, but it's natural to be afraid. You may struggle at first, but you can do this. You've got this."

Kaysen didn't appear convinced, but he nodded. "Sure."

"You don't believe me."

"No, but you were in my place, so you know. I trust you, but my belly doesn't."

He hugged his son. "I get it, but it will get better." He understood a whole lot more than Kaysen realized. He'd been working at dating apps and even appraising the men he'd seen when he went out on errands. He'd heard the chatter at the school about his situation and it scared him.

Good gravy. What if he met the wrong guy? Or something like Gil happened again? He'd never be able to live with himself.

The idea of getting out there freaked him out.

"Dad?"

"Yeah?"

He needed to get out of his own head. "What's up?"

"I'm ready to go." Kaysen hugged him again. "Thanks."

"No problem." He'd do pretty much anything for his son. "You're ready?"

"I am." Kaysen let go. "You're smart, Dad."

"I try." He swatted Kaysen on the butt. "Get your stuff. We're right on time."

"Which is pretty much close to being late." Kaysen shook his head. "Let's go."

"I thought you might say that." He collected the last of his belongings and followed Kaysen out of the kitchen. He locked the door, then headed into the garage.

Kaysen sat on the passenger seat and buckled up.

He joined his son in the car. As the garage door opened, Kaysen fidgeted with the vents.

"Need more air?" He'd turn on the stronger venting. "I can adjust it."

"No."

"Talk to me." Something was still off with Kaysen. "You can talk to me. Need some more words of wisdom? I can make something up." He tended to over-talk when the silence got to be too much, which used to piss Gil off.

"No." Kaysen stopped fiddling. "Are you going to date someone?"

"That's the plan, but I don't have a timeline." He backed out of the garage, then put the door down. "Why do you ask?"

"Mrs. O'Brien said she'd heard you were dating a guy from River Rock and asked me if I liked him."

"If I'm dating someone, then I don't know it. I don't think I've met anyone from River Rock." He backed into the turnaround, then headed down the driveway and onto the street. "If I'm interested in someone, I'll get your opinion. I value what you think."

"Thanks, Dad."

"Anytime. It's the truth." He drove across town toward the ballfield complex. Every time he arrived at the campus, the sheer volume of field space overwhelmed him. Fourteen ballfields on the twenty acres. There were spaces for picnicking and multiple spots for watching the various games. He turned his attention to his son. "So you've got that party or whatever between games. What are you all going to do? I never heard. Whitcomb was kind of vague."

"He's going to talk about the plays and strategies. Where we screwed up and how we can get better."

"Isn't that what Coach will do?"

"Not when Mr. Whitcomb thinks he's a better coach. I don't listen to him because he makes no sense," Kaysen said. "It's basically a lot of throw the ball to Dino and make him look good. Most of the team plays along with this, in theory."

"What about you?"

"I don't. I pretend. Most of us do that. Dino isn't bad—he's good, but he can't make every play. It's like me wanting to try to make every play. It's not possible and not smart baseball. We all need to do our best—not just one of us."

"Very true." And perceptive. His son had been paying attention. "Just keep your head on."

"As long as Mr. Whitcomb doesn't think we're not paying attention, we're fine. It's when he can tell we're not going along with the play that he gets angry and loud."

"Mind if I send a spy in to watch him?" He had a couple people he could ask to keep an eye on the situation without being so obvious. He pulled into the sports complex. "Do you have to stay there? Can you leave?"

"Bathroom break?"

"Sure."

"If we have to, then I want to. I'll take that excuse."

"I'm in the concession stand," Bram said. "If you want to visit to get away, please do. I don't want you to get into trouble, but I don't want you having to listen to garbage if it's not helping you."

Kaysen nodded. "I know what to do. You've taught me well."

"Good. Have the game you deserve. I'll be right behind you," Bram said. "You'll do just fine. Breathe and let yourself relax."

"Got it." Kaysen rushed out of the vehicle and in seconds, he stood at the trunk to retrieve his bag.

Bram shook his head. His son had grown too fast. One day, he wouldn't need his father any longer.

He hoped that day never came.

He left the car and grabbed his bag from the backseat, then hit the button to pop the trunk lid. Kaysen scooped up his bag and left without a word.

Bram snorted. *Kids.*

"Bram." Caleb Whitcomb strode up to him. "Hello."

Now it made more sense why Kaysen got away so fast. "Hello." The other parents on the team referred to him as Mr. Rode because the kids did from school. Caleb usually referred to him as Mr. Rode, so this had to be intentionally dismissive.

"So we're doing a team-building situation today between games. Do you want to join in?"

He really should, but he had a prior commitment. "I'm working the concession stand from two until four."

"Oh, so Klane conned you."

"Conned me?" He didn't understand. "He asked me for help and I agreed."

"He got to you." Whitcomb snorted. "I knew he would."

"Why?"

"He needs to stay neutral."

"Agreed." Where was Whitcomb going with this? "So?"

"He can't be neutral if he's leaning on certain parents."

"I needed to take a turn volunteering. It was my turn. Big deal."

"It should be that way, but we know the truth."

"I don't know the truth." He frowned and paused before speaking. "You think you can run the team better than Klane, don't you?"

"I know I can. He's wasting talent."

"They're in junior high school."

"And he's got two players that are attracting scouts," Whitcomb said. "Dino and Billy."

"I suppose." He'd paid attention to both players and neither set the world on fire. If he had to choose, he wouldn't put any one or two players above the rest of the team, and no scout was looking at junior high school students. The scouts wanted the players to develop. Besides, Dino needed to stop phoning in his plays. He didn't put in the effort he could, rather he was riding on what he'd already accomplished.

"You see it and get it. I thought you might, because you're smart." Whitcomb nodded. "Good, good. You'll stay out of it, though?"

"I'm not in it."

"Good." Whitcomb beamed. "I hoped you would see things that way."

"I just want to help the team. If it's in the stands, then I will. I trust Coach Klane, though. He deals with the team in the same ways my coaches did. He knows what he's doing and you should give him a chance."

Whitcomb's smile vanished. "Wait. Your coaches? Did you have a private coach for Kaysen?"

"No. I played ball."

"When?"

"College. I was scouted."

"No. Way."

"Way." He swore they sounded like they were in junior high school, not parents.

"Why aren't you doing the coaching?"

"Don't want to. I want to watch my son." He'd had enough to do without trying to run the team.

"But you'd be great."

"Klane's a great coach and he's doing fine. Now, excuse me, I need to catch up to Kaysen. He's waiting for me." It was a lie, but he didn't care. He needed to get away from Caleb Whitcomb.

He picked up his pace and strode to the field. Kaysen waited by the fence.

"I forgot to tell you he wanted to talk to you," Kaysen said. "Sorry."

"It's okay. Just worry about you. I've got that in hand."

"Okay." Kaysen hugged him before going to the dugout.

He sighed. He'd have to stay the hell away from Caleb for a while. He disliked Caleb's parenting style — hovering and demanding. Kids needed to be more independent and fail occasionally. They wouldn't grow if they didn't mess up or fall down every so often.

Deion rushed up to him. "Have you seen Alan?"

"No. Why? Is there something wrong?" He paid closer attention. "Is he not here?"

"He's here, but he got summoned by the superintendent. Is his contract in jeopardy?" Deion asked, breathless.

"Not that I know of, but I can see what I can find out." He wasn't sure what he was supposed to learn.

Still, he'd do his best and as soon as possible. Deion was a vital part of the team and if he was worried, then there had to be something big brewing. "Keep running the warm-ups and I'll be right back," Bram said. "I'll sort this out."

"Thanks." Deion nodded once, then drifted away.

Alan strode out of the field area toward the media box above the stands. Bram spent far too much time with Miguel Perez, the superintendent. Miguel was a predictably nice guy and well-suited for his side job doing the commentary for the sporting events for the school social media channels.

He rushed up the stairs to the second floor. When he knocked on the door, Miguel answered.

"Hi." Miguel crooked his brow, but grinned. "You're not the one I expected to see up here. Coming to help me?"

"I needed to speak to you. Do you have a minute?" This wasn't his normal approach to talking to the super, but this wasn't a normal conversation.

"Sure." Miguel ushered him into the press box. "No one else is here yet."

"Not Alan?"

"Come again?"

He should've referred to Alan by his last name. "I mean Mr. Klane—Coach Klane. Is he here?"

"No. I haven't seen him. What's wrong? Is he running late?" Miguel asked. "I can call Deion."

"Deion's here, but he was told you were looking for Coach." His heart hammered. Why was he so worried about Alan? Because he kind of liked him, but he didn't want the team to suffer.

"Nothing to sweat. He's not here and I don't need to see him," Miguel said. "Why would I need him? He's got a game to coach."

"Deion was told you needed Alan because you wanted to talk about his contract." The whole idea was silly because contracts were handled by the board, not the superintendent alone.

"His baseball contact goes for another year, but I'm recommending to the board that he gets another three-year one at the end of this one as an extension. We're lucky to have him," Miguel said. "If I could convince him to come back to teaching, I would."

"He'd be good."

"Agreed." Miguel folded his arms. "I never asked him, but now that you bring it up, I wonder if this was why Mr. Whitcomb stopped me."

"He wants Klane gone."

"He does."

"Do you know why?"

"He feels it's unfair." Miguel sighed and leaned on the counter. "His son isn't getting the attention he feels he should be and believes Klane is holding him back."

"He's not."

"I agree. The team is pretty balanced."

"It's sour grapes."

"You don't say…" Miguel snorted. "He didn't sway me, if that's what you're wondering."

"Good to hear. I have your word on this?" He wanted to be sure.

"You do. You can even vouch for him at the contract talks. I'd love it if you did."

"I can, yes." He barely knew Alan, but he refused to let him get hosed over.

"We start play in fifteen minutes. Where are my student assistants?" Miguel asked. "They should be here."

"I'll leave you to the game, so hopefully you find them soon. Enjoy the play calling and commentary. You're good, rookie." He shook hands with Miguel.

"Rookie." Miguel laughed. "I haven't been a rookie in years."

"I know." He shrugged and grinned, the left the room. As he hustled down the stairs, he spotted Alan. "Alan?" He rushed across the walkway. The more he tried to catch up to Alan, the faster Alan seemed to move. "Al?" He shouldn't call Alan by that shortened name, but he needed to get his attention.

Alan didn't stop or even slow down. Hell, he went even faster.

"Alan Klane." He broke into a jog, then run. After a moment, Bram caught up to him. "Hey. I need to talk to you."

Alan whipped around and his eyes blazed. "Oh." The fury in his eyes seemed to wane. "I'm sorry."

"It's fine," he puffed. "I needed to speak to you. I heard you needed to speak with Miguel."

"What'd he say? The man has it in for me and I'm tired of it. I did nothing," Alan said. "I coach, I encourage, I make them practice. Whoever does well does so because they put in the work and practice. If they don't, I try to work with them, but I can't make them all fantastic. Some are into self-sabotage."

"Slow down. I have an idea who upset you, but you've got the wrong idea. I don't want you to talk about it right here. Too many eyes. Come here." He grasped Alan's wrist and tugged him to the overhang by the bleachers. "I talked to Miguel and what he has to say isn't bad."

"Really?" Alan snapped. "You have no idea."

"Apparently I don't, but the point is that Miguel is putting you forward to get your coaching contract extended."

"What?"

"Unless you don't want that." He hadn't considered that.

"I—wait, what?"

"I'll vouch for you at the referral."

"Wait. Are you sure?"

"Yes. What or who has gotten you upset?"

"First, I had no idea. Second, you're too nice to find that out and I appreciate it. Third, I was under the impression I was in trouble and about to be fired. What happened?" Alan asked. "What'd I miss?"

"A lot," he replied. "You're not being fired, but there's someone gunning for you—as you know. Miguel and I won't let it happen." He'd made plenty of other mistakes, but not on this.

"You'd do that for me?"

"Sure." Without a doubt.

"Look, we all work for the same team, despite what some think. We need to stay on the same side." He nodded. "Now go coach that game. We've got this and we're playoff bound. We can't do that without you."

Alan grinned. "You have too much faith in me."

"Maybe, but I don't agree—it's merited. You do a good job."

"Thanks." Alan hesitated. "You're going to be in the stands?"

"Sure will. I look forward to working beside you in the concessions later, too." He winked, then walked away. He shouldn't have dismissed him so quickly, but Alan needed to get to the game.

Bram returned to the car to get his chair and cooler before heading to the grass beside the stands. He didn't mind sitting among the other parents, but being so tall, he liked being able to stretch his legs and not obstruct anyone's view if he stood. The stands had been built for shorter people, and he felt too compacted.

"Hi, Mr. Rode," one of his students said as she ran by and waved.

"Hi, Mattie." He would've said more, but Mattie was long past him by now.

He set up his chair and arranged his belongings while waiting for the game to begin. As the National Anthem played, he noticed a couple of other men enter the stands.

Nothing about the men said they were interested in him or even gay, but the longing took hold. He wanted to be held, kissed and loved. He missed being part of a couple.

He sighed and sat down at the end of the song. He shouldn't be thinking about relationships right now. He should be focusing on his son and having a life. Relationships, despite wanting to date, had to be on the back burner.

He watched the team run onto the field and Alan caught his attention. The guys had been cute, but seeing Alan in that uniform was nothing like he'd expected.

The uniform fit too well. He'd seen Alan in the team's colors plenty of times. How could he not? Alan was the coach. But seeing him now... The fit accentuated Alan's thin frame and moderate height.

It had to be the loneliness and lack of sex driving his thoughts, but Alan looked good.

He paid attention to the game. Kaysen's first few pitches didn't quite hit the mark. Bram stood and made his way to the fence.

"Breathe, Kay. Calm. Just pretend you're at the house and we're playing catch," he called. "You've got this."

Kaysen didn't react, but he seemed to get the message. His pitches were fine, being more strikes than going too wide right or left.

Bram settled back on his chair. So much for ogling Alan.

Note to self—pay attention to your son.

He focused on the game, watching Kaysen get out of the first inning and survive through to the sixth inning. His pitches hit the strike zone more often than not, and he'd only given up one run.

Not too bad for being thirteen and a young starting pitcher.

By the seventh inning, Alan switched Kaysen out for Dino, then Dino for Jinx. The team managed to get out of the seventh, but with two more runs given up.

His nerves frayed when the Panthers fell behind four to three. "Come on, guys," he muttered. "You can do this. Two runs. You just need two runs."

He tensed as the Panthers got one run, tying it up.

Kaysen wasn't the strongest hitter, but he did have power when he got the right pitches. Bram crossed his fingers that the pitcher would get precise enough with his throws for Kaysen to get a hit.

Kaysen swung, missing the first pitch, but connected with the second one and sent it deep into right field. The outfielder missed the ball, allowing Kaysen to make the pop fly into a double.

"There you go!" Bram shouted. "That's it." He didn't care if Kaysen scored. Kaysen had been able to get on base and stretch it into a double. Not too bad. Plus, after pitching in this game, he'd get a rest instead of playing in the next one. He'd earned the run and rest.

By the ninth inning, the score was still tied and Bram worried about the outcome. He shoved his worries aside. The outcome would be what it would be.

Bram waisted as the crowd thinned for the Panthers. He'd seen this before. If the team wasn't winning, parents tended to wander away. But if they were winning by a lot, every armchair coach had to witness the miracle. When they were losing, no one wanted to see it.

The final pitch came back to the plate and the Panthers player connected. The ball sailed over the head of the outfielder and over the fence.

Bram laughed as Miguel, in the press box, called the play. Miguel's voice raised an octave and Bram swore he heard Miguel jumping up and down.

Bram applauded and stood. He'd seen close games before, but this walk-off was great. His son had pitched a good, solid game and got the win.

Kaysen ran to the fence and threw his arms around Bram, despite the chain link between them. "You were right, Dad. I settled down, pretended we were in the yard playing catch and it worked. I got the win."

"You did." He ruffled Kaysen's hair. "Celebrate. You deserve it."

"You told me what to do and I did it."

"Thank your coach. He helped you as much," Bram said. "I'm proud of you."

"Thanks, Dad." Kaysen beamed. "I'll find you at the concession stand."

"You bet. Try to enjoy the team thing," he said. "Do your best."

"Mr. Whitcomb is mad we didn't run away with it," Kaysen said and shrugged. "He can talk. I'll ignore. Big deal."

"Do what you need to." He clapped Kaysen on the shoulder. "Focus on *your* game."

"I will." Kaysen adjusted his hat and hustled away.

Bram grinned. He shook his head and collected his belongings. He carried the chair, bag and cooler to the car before heading to the concession stand. There, he joined Shelley and Mark at the popcorn machine. "If you've ever used one of these things once, you remember it forever."

"You do," Shelley said. "You've done all those jobs, haven't you? You don't have to be here. Watch your kid."

"I'm a team player." He offered a sheepish grin. "I do what's expected."

"You do, and that's why you're special," Mark said. "We're glad when you help."

"Do you know you're the only admin that helps us more than once?" Shelley asked.

"It's not difficult and helps the community, so I don't mind." He'd help more if he had the time.

"Why don't you fill the popcorn boxes, then, and Mark will get the next batch started," Shelley said. "Since you're so willing to help. The next game is about to start and the one that was going on is about done, so we'll be slammed. Congrats on Kaysen's win. He deserved it."

"You've got it, and thank you." He set about filling the red and white boxes. "Kaysen worked hard."

"He did and so do you," Shelley said. "Tell me you're not allowing a matchmaker to set you up."

"What?" He dropped the scoop in the machine. "Sorry?"

"Don't let a matchmaker find you a date. Do it yourself or just let it happen," Shelley said. "There's one who wants you on her books so she can brag about it."

He'd expected that. "I'm not using a matchmaker. I have a partner to wade into the dating pool with."

"You do?" Mark nodded as he turned on the popper. "Smart. Who'd you pick? Tell me it's Alan. You both deserve to be happy."

"Yes." He'd lied, but he didn't care. In this moment, he needed the lie. No one would check him on this. If they asked Alan, he'd probably get embarrassed and defer. By then, he'd talk to Alan and shore up the story.

"Good. He's cute," Shelley said. "You should date him."

"Shel." *Jesus.* "He's my son's coach. But we're trying something." Good God. He kept digging himself in deeper. He needed to stop.

"That's fantastic. Alan is a good coach and I like what he's doing with the team. If he can help you, then I hope he does."

"Me, too." He resumed filling boxes, but this time with the fresh popcorn. He had to keep his mouth shut. He'd say something to the wrong person and get himself into more trouble.

A rush of people approached the stand. Bram refilled the candy slots and popcorn while Mark and Shelley handled sales. He preferred things this way. He was no salesman.

Within a few minutes, the rush trickled down. Bram refilled the popcorn popper with kernels and oil. The door opened.

Alan ducked into the room. "Hi."

"You're here early." Shelley rested her hands on her hips. "It's my go time. I need to get over to watch Len play. I never get to see the games. Are you taking over for me?"

"Yes." Alan accepted the apron. "Go. They just started."

"I'll never get to see the first pitch." Shelley shook her head before rushing out of the stand.

Mark frowned. "Where's Whitcomb?"

"With the team. They're doing a team-building activity," Alan said. "He's supposed to be working?"

Bram patted his back pocket. "I can get Todd to help. He's here with his family and would jump in if you need to be somewhere, Mark." He hoped he could get the high school vice principal to help. It was worth asking.

"I'll see if he comes by," Mark said. "But I have the feeling Whitcomb knew what he was doing and he's being a pain in my butt. I need to find a replacement, though. Let me talk to Andew. He's on field one watching his daughter. I'll be right back."

"We'll manage," Alan said. "No problem. Take your time."

"Thanks." With that, Mark left them alone in the room.

Once the door closed, Alan faced him. "I guess it's just you and me."

"It is." He shored up his courage. "I need to talk to you."

"Oh? What's wrong? Kay?" Alan asked. "He pitched well once he settled."

"He did, but this is about us. I might have implicated us." *Might* was the wrong word. He'd gone too far, but he'd gotten flustered. When he got nervous, his words jumbled and he seemed to lose the ability to properly express himself.

"Oh?" Alan repeated and paled. "In what?"

"Having a relationship." There. He'd said it. He swore the oxygen left the room. What would Alan say about that?

Shit.

Chapter Five

Alan stared at Bram. He'd had so many things go wrong today, but this wasn't on his bingo card. He needed Bram to repeat what he'd said. "What?"

"I thought you might be upset," Bram said.

"Upset?" No, he wouldn't say that. "Mystified is more like it."

"Not shocked."

He shook his head and held up his hand. There was so much to wade through. "Wait."

"Yes?"

"Why'd you say it? What possessed you to declare it?" He wanted to understand. "We barely know each other."

"I know." Bram hesitated. "It was impulsive."

"I guess." He noticed the way Bram fidgeted and shifted his weight from his left to his right foot. He wasn't used to seeing Bram so off-balance. This must've been a shock to him, too. He wanted to yell, but that wasn't going to solve anything. He needed to use some tenderness. "So what happened?"

"I said you and I were in a relationship of sorts," Bram said. "So we're kind of together. I'm making a huge mess of this, no matter how much I try to explain. It happens when I'm nervous. Sorry."

The news mentally knocked him on his ass. "We... You..." He wasn't sure what to say. He did want to see Bram. Being with him was one of his goals. But like this? It seemed so odd.

Also sort of fitting.

He and Bram probably wouldn't have made any moves on their own. They needed a bit of pushing to get here.

"Are you angry?" Bram asked. "I understand if you are, but I'd very much take any dating help I can get."

"I'm not much better off." He massaged his temples. "Where are the parents? Shouldn't we be selling shit right now?" He'd slipped and used blue language, but it'd slipped out.

"Language."

He had to give that to Bram. "Sorry."

"It's fine. I screwed up and I'll fix it. I said what I said under pressure, but that doesn't make it right." Bram thrust his fingers into his hair. "I'm terrible when cornered."

"No, you're not."

Bram's eyes widened.

"You're pretty great when the heat's on, but I'm guessing you don't like heat about your personal life. I'm terrible when I'm pressed on that myself." Alan sighed. He needed a few minutes to process what he'd been told. It made sense, but was still so impossible. He and Bram were together, in a way, and he kind of liked it. They could also just move on from this and not let it go anywhere, if they so chose. But, he wanted to go out with him for real and try a relationship.

"You can argue and I'll go along with it," Bram said. "I see we're about to get customers and I haven't put hotdogs on the rollers."

"We'll get it." Alan filled the machine with a row of hotdogs, then added butter to the freshly popped corn. He could work under pressure when needed. "We'll talk about this later."

"I put you in a bad position because of my mouth." Bram bowed his head. "I expect people to act with decorum and I can't even do it."

"It's fine." Alan put the scoop down. "We'll figure it out."

"Alan."

"Maybe it's not as bad as you think." Alan resumed prepping the stand. Customers did arrive and expected service. While Bram handled sales, Alan filled orders. Alan liked the way they worked together. They'd fallen into a rhythm quickly and barely needed to talk to help each other.

Maybe they were good together.

Yes, he was upset that Bram had told a tale, but what if they did try to have a relationship? If they went into a dating situation and it worked? Would that be so bad?

Maybe, but maybe not.

Mark finally returned to the stand. "I can't find help when I need it and have to turn it away when I don't. If it's raining, everyone wants to help me. It's a beautiful day, so no one's interested."

"Want me to text Todd?" Bram asked.

"Nope. I saw him in the stands. He's here long enough for his girl to play, then he's back home. His wife is at a conference and their older boy is sick." Mark put an apron on. "I'm here for the duration."

"I can stay," Bram said. "Kay won't be playing in the second game, which means I'll be here while he encourages his team, so I'm free."

Alan admired Bram's dedication. "You're right. He's got to rest."

"I can't leave because I won't leave him here, but that means you can have me." Bram smiled and counted change for a customer. "I'll help."

"I'd help, but I need to get back to coaching," Alan said. "I can help a little longer, though." He patted his hip, expecting his phone to ring or buzz with messages from Deion. There hadn't been any word yet, which bothered him. He wanted information because his team had been hijacked.

"Are you okay?" Bram asked.

"Yeah." He shook his head. If Mark thought he and Bram were close, then he had to keep up that appearance. Part of him wanted to be annoyed, but the rest of him was thrilled. He liked Bram's company.

"What's wrong?" Bram cornered Alan by the popcorn machine. "Is it me?"

"No." He shook his head. "Not everything is about you."

Bram recoiled. "I figured I made a huge declaration and messed everything up. I thought I'd pissed you off. I'm sorry."

He needed some calm. Bram had a good point, but no one was trying to be careless right now. "I'm upset because my team is being hijacked and I'm worried."

"You won't believe me, but it's not as bad as you think."

"No?" He'd love to hear why.

"The team doesn't listen to him."

He paused. "For real?"

Bram nodded. "They pick and choose but tend to ignore him. They know what's what and trust your coaching. They give him enough that he thinks he's got them, but they do what you ask when the heat's on."

That helped—if it was true. He needed to believe him, though, because he doubted Bram would lie about this. He might lie about other things, but not something so important.

"They trust you," Bram said. "Their play shouldn't change now after this meeting." He lowered his voice. "Kay says they pretend and play along, then go back to what you teach them because as Kay says, he doesn't know what he's talking about."

He should be reassured, but he wasn't. There was a loud, cranky monster coming into his domain to cause trouble. His team was on the verge of making the playoffs. Hell, if a couple of the other teams playing today lost, they might already be in and have that third seed, but not know it. But time was being wasted as Whitcomb bullied and brayed about what he wanted from the team.

Alan wanted the same thing every other coach did— cooperation, hard work and determination on the part of the players. That wasn't too much to ask.

"What time do you need to get to the field?" Bram asked.

The question confused Alan for a moment. He checked his watch. "I have a few minutes."

"Why don't you go? You could get a glimpse of what was going on? I'd planned on asking a friend to snoop, but I got sidetracked and forgot."

"It happens." He clapped Bram on the shoulder. "Your heart was in the right place." That seemed to be the sentiment all the way around. Bram wasn't trying to be a jerk. He wanted the best for everyone—just like a principal would.

He untied the apron and left it on the counter. "I'll go. I need to put on a fresh jersey."

"You look fine," Bram said.

"You don't have to keep selling it," Alan said. "I'm on your side."

Something in Bram's eyes lit a fire in Alan. The grin on his lips not only illuminated Bram's face, but gave him an aura. Alan couldn't look away. If Alan had to admit it, he liked the pushing and the fire. He'd made a move and didn't regret it.

"I'll find you after the game," Bram said. "We could get dinner?"

"I'd like that." It'd give them a chance to figure out what they were doing. "I'll see you."

"You will."

Alan hurried away toward the field. If he lingered too long, he might try to touch Bram again, or even kiss him. It was too soon. He needed to slow down and get to know Bram. He'd begun to fall for the sexiness of the man in a position of power. He liked the way Bram looked in those suits and how he carried himself.

But now he needed to get to know the real man, the father and the partner he could be.

He strode to the dugout to the bag he'd tucked behind the coach's chair. There wasn't anything of importance in the bag, short of a change of shirt and stick of deodorant. He kept his wallet, phone and keys with him at all times, in case anyone besides Deion rummaged through the bag.

Deion rushed into the dugout. "Thank God. I'll get the team."

He wanted to ask what Deion meant, but Deion left before he could get the question formed in his mind. He switched out of the sweaty jersey and into the clean one. As he buttoned the front, Deion returned.

"I've got them in the outfield warming up," Deion said. "But we've got to talk."

"Sure. I'll follow you to the field."

"Can you get Whitcomb tossed from the complex?"

That stopped him. "Tossed?"

"He wants to sit in on this game."

"Sorry. I'll be happy to tell him no myself. We can't have unauthorized people on the field during actual play. He's not on the list and I'm not getting the game scratched because he's in a mood."

"I know that."

"He doesn't. If he did, then he'd also know it'll screw with Dino's averages." He left the dugout and spotted Caleb on the warning track. "Mr. Whitcomb?"

Caleb beamed. "It's going to be a great game."

"It may be, but I need a word with you." He stood between Caleb and the field. "I hear you're wanting to stand in on this game."

"Yes. The boys need me."

"That may be, but I can't allow that."

"Why?" Caleb shot back, glaring. "You do realize they need me."

"They may, but I have to submit a list of personnel for the team and you're not on it. I have to let the league know who is permitted to be here and who isn't."

Caleb's eyes blazed and he opened his mouth to argue, but Alan held up his hand. "You need to go. Why? Because if anyone is seen on the field who isn't on the list, then the officials can demand either you leave or we forfeit the game. Which do you want?"

"Amend the list."

"I can't. I had to submit it back before the season started."

"Oh, for God's sake."

"It might not be fair, but we really don't want to forfeit. Your son is starting the game. If we have to give the game away, then he's going to get the loss. You don't want that on his record, do you?"

Caleb's eyes darkened. His brow furrowed, but he nodded and forced a smile. "I suppose you're right."

"You tell me to keep an eye out for Dino and how things look to the scouts. This is me doing just that," Alan said. "I want him to succeed."

"Sure."

"He won't get to pitch again in the regular season if you stay where you are."

"But he will in the postseason?"

"If we get in."

"We will. He got us there."

Alan gritted his teeth. "I'm waiting for final confirmation."

"He got us there." Caleb finally relaxed a bit. "If it gets him extra chances, then I'll go. He deserves to have his work recognized. I expect he'll be the team MVP again this year."

"The players decide that, not me."

"Then they'll vote for him." With that, Whitcomb turned on his heel and walked away.

Alan kept an eye on him until he was off the field. His heart raced and he wiped his palms on his pants legs. Why did some people have to be so irritating?

Deion joined him by the fence. "We good?"

"We're good." He kept watching until Caleb found a seat in the stands. "I'm pretty sure he's not satisfied and feels I've slighted his child, but I can't focus on the team if I'm worrying about this."

"Nope." Deion swatted Alan's hip. "Let's strategize. We need to get ready for the game."

"Yeah." He left the fence and walked with Deion to the dugout. "How'd it go?"

"As expected. He railed against what you taught them. Follow what he says instead. He kept talking about Dino and the scouts. When the people look at them, tell people about Dino. You never know who the scouts are, so build up Dino. He said so much about his son and how we have to cater to Dino. Throw to him, hit to him, let him make the play. What's worse? Dino's tired of it. He's missing catches and throws that I know he can make."

"Why?"

"He wants to be thrown off the team."

"Interesting." He wanted Dino to start this game, but not if he felt fatigued—physically or emotionally. "I'll talk to him."

"Probably best."

"Run practice and the warm-up for me and I'll get him ready for pitching."

"Done." Deion nodded once and headed to the outfield with the players.

Alan glanced back at the media stand. Underneath was the concessions area. No doubt Bram was still there helping. He couldn't stop himself from grinning at the memory of working beside Bram. It was silly. They weren't really a thing, but they were going to have supper together after the game. That had to mean something.

Plus, Bram had a nice body. He wanted to hug and caress him. Kiss and cuddle, touch and explore. But right now, he needed to focus on anything except Bram and their time together. He sighed and ambled to the other end of the dugout. "Dino."

"I'm in trouble," Dino said.

"Who said that?" He leaned on the wall and faced Dino. He crossed his ankles. "You're not in trouble."

"Why not? My Dad doesn't want you to be my coach. How can that not mean trouble?"

"That's what he wants, but it's not what this is about. What do you think?" he asked. "You have a voice here."

"I do?" Dino's eyes widened and he stared at Alan. "I'm a kid."

"And you're my pitcher."

"One of them."

"Can't have you pitch in every game. You'd be tired and never recover. You'd hate it."

"I hate playing," Dino muttered.

"Why?" He knelt down, getting onto Dino's level. "What makes you hate playing?"

"Dad."

"Oh?" He'd expected this.

"I can't tell you."

"You can. You need a safe place to speak, and this is one." He focused on Dino. "Talk to me."

Dino sighed. "You won't get mad?"

"Nope."

Dino didn't speak right away. He fidgeted with his glove. "I don't like baseball."

"That's okay."

"It is?" The true shock in Dino's voice struck Alan.

"It is, and you don't have to love the game. Some don't. It may not be in your blood." He sat on the wall and laced his fingers together. "There are days when I'm not a fan of the game. When I had a rough stretch, I'd get discouraged."

"Did you want to quit?"

"No, but I couldn't imagine not playing the game, either. It was in my blood. That said, when I was thirteen, I wasn't being pushed the way you are."

Dino sighed. He frowned and tossed his glove onto the bench. "I want to quit because I want to play football. It's more fun, but Dad says I can't because I'll get hurt."

"You could."

Dino rolled his eyes. "Not you, too."

"I'm not going either direction. I'm simply agreeing you could get hurt. Sports can cause injury."

"Oh."

"Why else?"

"Dad pushes so hard," Dino said. "The guys hate me because he makes them feel badly if they don't throw to me. They hate that he makes a big deal about me. I'm not good." His voice cracked.

The pain in his words and attitude bugged Alan. This wasn't fair. "You do have talent."

"I do?"

"Sure. You need to cultivate it, but if you don't love the game, then you won't want to do that. I'd like you to play the game because you want to. Do what makes you happy. If you can't make the play, then don't. If you can, then good. If it's in left field and you're in right, then there's nothing to it—let the left fielder get it."

"You're not mad?"

"No. I want my players to be happy."

"Dad's angry I'm not the MVP right now. He says I'm not trying enough."

"Then try hard enough for you. You're pitching this afternoon. Do your best and remember, we're in the playoffs. Every win counts."

"We are?"

"Yeah, so play like it's all fun because it is right now. Let's have fun with this game."

"Okay." Dino brightened. He hopped up from his seat. "I'm sorry Dad gets intense. He does it with everyone. You should see him with Delia's gymnastics coach." He rolled his eyes, then left the dugout and headed toward the mound to warm-up.

Alan bowed his head. He should've known Caleb would be tough on everyone. Dino's sister Delia was a skilled gymnast, but if she was being pushed too hard, too, then he'd bet she was tired as well.

The umpires strode onto the field while his players hustled to the first base line. He gestured the players into the dugout for his standard pre-game speech. Halfway through, he changed his mind.

"Panthers, we've made the playoffs. We'll keep going beyond today, but does that mean we write the game off? Nope. We play it like every other game. It still counts. We're all on the same team and we've worked hard, but we still need to have fun. Play like this is a pickup game in the backyard. Have fun and bring it in." He held his hand out.

As all the other hands came into the center, he shouted. "Play like it's fun, enjoy the game. We're the Panthers. One-two-three...Panthers!"

"Panthers," the team shouted in unison.

His players hustled back to the field, assuming their positions.

He might not have been able to please the many people in his life, but he swore he could coach a team. Win or lose, he got them this far and he believed in them. They could go the distance.

Now it was time for them to give the game their best.

Alan coached the team like he had with the first clash. Like the first matchup, this one wasn't easy. The Ravens gave the Panthers a hard time in the outfield. Anything his team managed to hit, the Ravens were able to catch. He'd been amazed by some of the diving catches. His players could've made the catches as well, but hadn't practiced for those events.

By the eighth inning, the score was only one to one, but that didn't ease his slight heartburn. Neither team had been sloppy in their play. They'd been very evenly matched.

He half-expected to hear from Caleb or other player parents about the game situation.

Deion folded his arms. "What do you think?"

"They're weaker on the left field side. We keep hitting long balls, but the third baseman and shortstop are getting bored. The outfield is tired. We need a few hits that stay in the infield or better yet, we need a bunt. Something to change it up."

"It's already the bottom of the eighth."

"I know." He stopped Jimmy before the young man went onto the field to hit. "Bunt."

Jimmy nodded. "Why?"

"Sean can run fast and we've only got one out. If you bunt, then he can put on speed. It'll confuse them because they want a power hit. We need to not do that. Throw them off."

Jimmy adjusted his helmet and flexed his hands on the bat. "You got it, Coach."

"Go get 'em." Alan clapped as Jimmy went to the plate. Keith had just gotten a single on a hit sent between the first and second basemen that landed shallow in the outfield.

As Alan expected, the mistake messed up the Ravens. Jimmy bunted on the second pitch, allowing Sean to sail to third and Keith to second. Jimmy put on extra speed, making it to first base before the throw.

"Bases loaded," Deion said. He fidgeted and rapped his knuckles on the wall. "Can we count on Dino?"

"He's the next one up. It's his shot." He winked at Dino. "Remember to have fun."

"Will do," Dino replied.

Alan stood stoic in the dugout. He'd taught them what to do, how to play and how to handle clutch situations, but now it was up to them to show what they'd learned.

Dino went to bat and let the first two pitches go. He swung hard at the third and connected, sending the ball into the outfield. The sacrifice fly was caught, causing the second out, but in the meantime both Sean and Jimmy were able to score.

Good enough.

Deion screamed. "Oh my God!"

"We have to hold it through the top of the ninth," Alan said, keeping his voice calm. Having two runs on their side did help, but it wasn't enough until the game was over.

He watched tensely as the Ravens fell apart in the ninth, failing to get a single hit. Before he realized it, the game was over.

"We did it." Deion scrambled onto the field to celebrate with the team.

Alan sank onto the bench. His knees buckled and he sighed.

"You did it," Bram said and joined him on the bench. "I listened to the commentary while I worked. I'm pretty sure Miguel doesn't have a voice now."

"We did. Not me, though. We. They really came through."

Bram matched his position as he sat beside him. "You've taught them well."

"I tried."

Bram patted Alan's thigh. "You should go out there with them and celebrate."

Electricity shot through him. He couldn't think straight. Not with Bram touching him. Words escaped him and he wanted this moment to keep going.

"Are you okay?" Bram asked. His eyes glittered. "You seem off-balance."

His tongue felt like it was about a foot thick. "I am," he managed. "Sorry."

"Don't be."

"I—celebrate—yeah." Good Lord, he sounded so silly. He had to get himself under control.

"Celebrate with the players and we'll get pizza," Bram said. "I'm not leaving without Kay, so go enjoy yourself."

"Yeah." He stood and wandered away from Bram, but he was still so wobbly. He managed to join the team for celebrations. The boys dumped a cooler of water on him, hitting mostly his lower back and rear end. He screamed. When he glanced back at Bram, the chill left him, replaced by a fire deep in his soul.

What would it feel like to have Bram hold him? Kiss him? Probably like heaven.

"All right, guys. Bring it in." He waited for them to huddle up on the mound. "We got the win and you all did well. I liked how we handled the clutch. We worked like a well-oiled machine, but this game is over and it's time to focus on the next game. We have a week until the next bout, but that also means we're not giving up. We're not quitting. We keep grinding because we're a unit and we keep it together. Panthers on three...one, two, three...Panthers!"

The boys shouted and whooped, then scattered to their various parents and family members.

Alan exhaled and hugged Deion. "We did a good job."

"We did." Deion laughed. "And it's just starting. We have a hard potential schedule ahead of us."

"We do, but one game at a time." He tensed. He'd much rather see Bram coming toward him, not Caleb Whitcomb. "Here we go."

Deion remained beside him. "Witnesses."

"Sweet." He straightened his spine to brace for the argument. "Mr. Whitcomb."

"I see you let him hit," Caleb said. "He won the game for you."

"For the team," Alan said.

"We all worked for this together," Deion said. "We adjusted the way we attacked the ball, noting weakness with the other team, and Dino took direction to exploit that weakness."

"He used my directions."

"Whoever told him, he used it and it helped," Alan said. "He has talent."

"I know," Caleb shot back. "When you focus properly on him, he excels."

"Mr. Whitcomb, we have to give every player the same treatment," Deion said. "He's one of the team and we work together."

"Just remember, I helped them before this win and I expect a chance to strategize with them before each playoff game," Caleb said. "I expect it."

"We have to play by the rules. I adhere very tightly to them," Alan said. "No question."

"We'll see." Caleb snapped his fingers, summoning Delia and Dino to leave. Once they were out of earshot, Alan exhaled and scrubbed the back of his hand across his mouth.

"I don't know what I can do about him," Alan said. "I swear. I need to find the exact rules for parental involvement before we jeopardize our shot at the playoffs. We could lose our seed if he meddles too much."

"I'll start checking the rules and asking the right people. We have a week, so we have some time," Deion said. "We'll sort it out." He turned his back to the crowd and chuckled.

"What?" Alan asked. "I could use a good joke right about now. What's so funny?"

"Your face," Deion said. "You're angry and red, but every time you glance at Bram—and yes, I see you looking—you turn a different shade of red. Did you make a move?"

"I kind of did," Alan admitted. "I'm going to have pizza with him and Kay tonight." It was a huge step to go with Bram, but an even bigger one to tell Deion the truth about it.

"You go, man!" Deion applauded. "I'm proud of you. Hit that."

"Deion." He tried to disguise his embarrassment, but secretly, he liked the encouragement. "Thanks."

"Here comes your man." Deion grinned. "Good luck."

He paid attention to Bram. Luck? He'd need so much more than luck. Grace, intelligence and patience would help.

Just don't screw this up.

Chapter Six

Bram carried Kaysen's bag as he approached Alan and Deion. He didn't want to interrupt the conversation, but he should speak to Alan. "Hi."

"Hi." Deion waved. "I need to go." He hurried away, leaving Bram and Alan alone.

"Did I prevent some huge strategy session?" Bram asked. "I can go."

"No." Alan reddened.

Was it a blush or a sunburn? Bram wasn't sure.

"We were done," Alan said. "It wasn't anything confidential."

"Oh, so game plans?"

"Not exactly." He inched up to Bram. "How can I help you?"

"I wanted to invite you to the house for pizza. Kaysen wants pizza, but he's tired and wants to go home, rather than to the restaurant. I ordered it in."

"You don't mind?" Alan asked. "It's not too forward?"

"We're supposed to be close, so it's fine." Besides, it was his idea. How was that too forward? It was expected, right? "I thought we could talk and strategize."

"About the game?" Alan groaned. "For once, I'm tired of baseball."

"I meant dating," Bram said. "Give me your phone." He understood what Alan meant, though. At some point during every ballplayer's life, they got a bit tired of the game. It was a matter of if the tiredness wore off.

Alan handed over the device.

"Here's my information—including my address. You can follow me there or show up when you're ready if you want to go home and get cleaned up first."

"I'll follow," Alan said. "I need to vent."

"Sure." Bram waved his hand. "I'm sure Kay will eat and crash. He's exhausted."

"I'm sure." He fell in step with Bram. "I'm sorry I'm grumpy."

"You just coached two games and worked the stand. I'd be shocked if you weren't tired."

Alan stopped by his beat-up truck. "Where is your car?"

"A couple rows back. The blue Caddy."

"High roller." Alan finally smiled. "I see it. I'll follow you."

"Are you sure?" If Alan wanted to change his mind, Bram would understand. The day had been a lot to take in.

"Positive." Alan winked. "I need good food and good times with good people."

He wouldn't disagree. "That's a lot of good."

"So are you." Alan hesitated before climbing behind the wheel of his truck. "Get your kid so we can go."

"Oh. Yeah." He'd left Kaysen in the car, not that Kaysen minded. He was probably on his phone. "You're following me?"

"I am." Alan grinned and the move temporarily disarmed Bram.

Bram wandered back to his car and slid behind the wheel. He needed a moment to regroup.

"Dad?"

"Yeah?" So much for regrouping.

"Is Coach coming with us?" Kaysen asked.

"I invited him, yes. I wanted to get to know him and felt having you there made the most sense." He noticed Alan's truck and decided he should head home. "Is that all right with you?"

"Just as long as he doesn't lecture me about my game play or tablet usage." Kaysen fiddled with his phone. "If he's normal, then fine."

"He should be." He got it, though. There were few things more irksome than having to rehash the game once it was over, or having someone who didn't have kids give parenting advice. "If he gives you grief, then you can change the subject or leave the room."

"I can disappear?"

He drove away from the sports complex. "Yes. You shouldn't, but I understand if you do." He'd prefer Kaysen not jump to conclusions or abandon him because his ego couldn't handle being left. He wanted the protection of his son there.

Terrible, but true.

He spied Alan behind him. At least that was working out.

"Want to order the pizza for me?" Bram asked. "I sort of told him I'd already ordered it. What do you want on yours?"

Kaysen took the phone from the console. "Can we get cheesy bread and the habanero ranch sauce?"

"Sure. Don't put it on his food to trick him, but yes. Get the regular, too."

"What do we want on the pizza this time?" Kaysen tapped the screen. "A large?"

"You get a medium with whatever you want on it. Get a large for Coach and me with pepperoni. That should work," Bram said.

"Thanks, Dad." Kaysen tapped the screen. After a moment, he paused. "Delivery or pickup?"

"Delivery. I'm tired of serving everyone else." He pulled onto their street. "I'm tired."

"You, too?" Kaysen finished up with the phone. "Okay. All ordered. Should be here in forty minutes. I paid and put the tip on the order already."

"Thanks." He only ever let Kaysen use his card for pizza. He stopped in the driveway and hit the fob for the garage door to open. "Put your gear bag in the bin and leave your cleats on the back patio. I'll hose them off later. Put your clothes in the washer, too. I need to get the stains out of your jersey."

"I do that every time, Dad. Use the stick, don't use too much, and don't add bleach."

"Correct." Kaysen's response both surprised and pleased him. He *had* been listening. He parked in the garage. Once he turned off the engine, he sighed.

"You really are tired, aren't you?" Kaysen asked and opened his car door. "I'm sorry."

"It's not your fault." He'd overbooked himself. "I'll be fine."

"Tell him to go home."

He'd forgotten for a moment that Alan was about to arrive. He noticed the truck behind him. *Crap.*

"You can," Kaysen said. "He'll be cool with it."

"He would, but I invited him. I should see this through." He did like Alan and wanted to give this a chance. "Maybe he'll help me find a date."

"According to the guys on the team, you and Coach are already dating."

He left the car and choked on his shock. So much for moving slowly. "We're not dating."

"Yet." Kaysen rolled his eyes as he kicked out of his cleats. "Dad, it doesn't matter to me."

"Yes, it does."

Kaysen stared at him. "Maybe it does, but I want my dad to smile again."

"What?" They had so much to talk about. "Kay?"

"You only smile the one way you use when you're at school. You don't smile because something's funny or silly. It's a plastic smile. Ever since Gil walked out, you don't smile, you force it."

He hadn't thought his son had noticed. "I'm sorry. I'll do better."

"If you have to think about smiling, then it's not genuine. I want my dad back," Kaysen said. "To laugh at my jokes, smile like you're happy and to relax. You don't ever relax."

Now, he wished he'd been a better actor. "Kay…"

"If Coach makes you laugh and it's real, then I'm all for it. But don't be fake." Kaysen shook his head. "I hate fake people. Girls like to say whatever they think will get a boy to pay attention and that's not how it should be. The boys do the same thing—they show off for the girls. If you like someone, then you don't have to do that. Just be yourself."

"You're right."

"So do that with Coach."

"Yes, sir." He couldn't argue with his son's logic. "You can disappear if you want to — especially if it's too much of a trainwreck."

"Good. I need to call Jess and tell her about the game."

"Jess?" This was new.

Kaysen rolled his eyes again, then pulled his jersey up over his head. "Jess Rockwell."

"I thought you were just friends."

"We are." Kaysen blushed like Alan had earlier. "We talk a lot."

"Oh. Well." He needed to learn so much about his son. "Get back to the kitchen when the pizza arrives and show up, but call her."

"Thanks." Kaysen ran off, leaving him in the garage.

Alan finally approached. "Hey."

"Hi."

"You seemed like you needed a moment with Kay, so I held back."

"He's got a special friend, I guess." He massaged his temples. "He's growing up too fast."

"They do. I bet if we called our mothers, they'd say the same thing about us."

"I'm sure." He could hear his mother now saying it. "I'm becoming my parents."

"Is that bad?"

"Not entirely." He popped the trunk again, retrieving the chair and cooler. "I never even touched this."

"Did you bring something good?"

"Water and sports drinks." The tips of his ears burned. "I should've brought a pack of energy chews or a fruit and nut pack for Kaysen. I forgot to replenish it all."

Alan stuffed his hands in his pockets. "Do you want me to postpone or cancel this?"

"What?" The question knocked him back a beat. "No. I want you to stay."

"Are you sure? You seem upset."

"I'm nervous."

"Why?"

"I haven't had a man over since my divorce and I forgot what it's like to invite someone over. I don't want to mess it up."

"You won't." Alan chucked. "Would you believe I'm nervous, too? I'm worried you'll change your mind."

"Why?" He admired how they were so similar in their fears. "You're a good guy. You must be — you had to pass the background check to work with students."

"That's not my issue."

"Then what is it?" He'd love to know.

"You're a principal and I'm a coach. I manage a sports club, but you're important. You should aim higher," Alan said. "Maybe that's what I should do — find you someone better. Really be your coach."

"Alan." The more Alan spoke, the more he'd come to like him. Alan's lack of confidence and his genuine concern were sweet. It made him more relatable.

"What? I can make a game plan for that. I can find you some good ones." Alan laced his fingers together behind his head. "We can figure this out."

"We can." He reached out and brushed his fingers across Alan's chest. "Stop."

"What?" Alan tensed and put his arms down.

"We can figure this out, but maybe we try dating each other?"

"Bram."

"Yes, I'm a principal and you're a coach, but so what? I heard you were a teacher. That's pretty cool. I'd like to get to know you better, and I'd bet you'd like to know more about my playing days. I want to know you and what makes you tick." He touched Alan's belly. "You're my type, by the way. Ask the support group. I like sporty guys."

"You're trying to be kind."

"Is it working?" he asked. "I'm authentic."

"I have no doubt."

"Then give me a chance. What do we have to lose? The chance at a relationship?"

Alan seemed to think about the questions. In the meantime, the pizza delivery driver pulled up in front of the house.

Bram side-stepped him and strode up to the driver. "Thank you. I put the tip on the bill."

"You did. Thanks." The driver offered over three boxes. "Have a good evening."

"We will." He carried the boxes up the drive to Alan's truck. "Come on. We have plenty and you need to eat. We deserve a break. Plus, the air's on, so we can cool down."

Alan followed Bram into the house.

"Sorry, it's messy. I haven't had a chance to clean up. Weekends aren't my best time," Bram said, wishing he'd gone through the house, picking up after himself. He wasn't a slob by any means, but still there were papers out, Kaysen's socks on the floor, and he should've run the vacuum.

"This is messy?" Alan kicked out of his sneakers. "I'd kill to have my apartment this clean."

"You don't pick up after yourself?" He didn't want another slob in his life.

"No, I'm just never home. I take care of the minimum and spend most of my time at the field or the club. I've got great managers, so I don't need to be there, but I don't know what else to do with myself."

That made sense. During conference time, he spent many hours at the school. "I get it."

Kaysen buzzed in and picked up his box, as well as half of the cheesy bread. "Thanks, Dad."

"Want to breathe a second before disappearing?" Bram asked.

Kaysen froze. "Sorry. Hi, Coach. I ordered the pizza, so I hope you like it."

"I haven't had a pie I didn't like, so it should be fine. Thanks," Alan said. "Good game. Enjoy the rest. You deserve it."

Kaysen eyed him a moment. "Thanks." He waited a second, then carried the food from the kitchen.

Bram shrugged. He opened the second box before getting plates. "I told him he could hide."

"He's tired."

Bram offered him a paper plate. "He was worried you'd want to talk about the game. My ex used to grill him and I'm sure he's hesitant."

"Wow." Alan held onto the plate and didn't reach for any food. "Why was he so rough?"

"Get something to eat. We'll talk in the living room. Kay's probably in the rec room watching videos of gaming."

"He likes those?"

"He decompresses with them. I have blocks up so he can watch some stuff, but not everything. I try to keep the lid on him to a degree." Bram filled his plate. "Water, milk, tea or soda? I think I have some beer and a bottle of wine."

"Tea is great." Alan got two slices of pizza. "I've never ordered from Besta Pizza Around."

"Kaysen loves them because they throw in extra sauce. Notice there's none in the box? Plus, he knows the family that runs the restaurant."

"Saucy."

"Cute." He put his plate down and poured two glasses of tea. "Here's the drink. I have napkins on the coffee table."

"Thanks." Alan hesitated. "Where is it?"

"This way. The house isn't all that big, but it's an odd floorplan. They made it windy and more like a maze." He directed Alan to the front room. "I don't use this space much. I'm either in my office over the garage or my room."

"You don't spend that much time with Kaysen?"

Bram realized what he'd said. "Goodness, I do. We're usually in the rec room and I hide out after he goes to bed."

"Makes sense."

"Have a seat." Bram settled on the sofa. "I never would've bought a white couch, but my ex wanted it. He said it was a show piece."

"More like a magnet for stains." Alan sat beside him. "So…"

"So." He put his glass down. "What's wrong?"

"Nothing, but my phone is blowing up."

"Texts?"

"Texts, messages, whatever. No one knew we were a couple and they're asking questions," Alan said. "Are we?"

Good question. He rested his plate on his lap. "I guess the first thing I should ask is, do you want to?"

"Be a couple?"

"Yes." Bram held his breath, fearful of Alan's reply.

"We shouldn't."

"I guess there are reasons why, but I can't think of any."

"Bram."

"Yes?" He perked up.

"I do like you. I enjoy your company," Alan said. "We made a good team in the stand."

"We did." They could in the sack, too. He knew it. "So, would you go out with me?" He might be rushing, but he didn't care.

"I would." Alan smiled. "Guess today is sort of a date, isn't it?"

"It is." Bram relaxed. "Sorry. My heart's been hammering. I thought you'd say no."

"I'm interested. Cautious, but interested." Alan finally nibbled on his pizza.

"I messed up," Bram said as he watched Alan. "I never asked if you were dairy sensitive. I'm slipping."

"I'm not." Alan sipped his tea. "This is good."

"Thanks. Came from a box." Bram faced Alan. "So what's your story? Or do you want to hear mine first?"

Alan laughed. "At least you start with the hard stuff. Get it out now so the rest is easier?"

"Yes. I can go first." He wasn't going to hide. Why? The story would come out, and he might as well steer it.

"Sure. How'd you end up divorced?" Alan asked.

"Gil and I met when we were in college. I played ball and he wanted to be on the team, but he didn't have it. I was smitten with him from the start, but I found out he wanted to be me — not be with me."

"That's cruel."

"It is, but I had no idea. I thought he liked me and I'd never dated anyone before, so I didn't see the signs." He wanted the whole story out on the table. "I couldn't see what he saw in me, but he liked me, so I kept the relationship going. The support group hated him."

"Support group? Your friends?" Alan asked.

"Yes, Dante, Tim and Josef. We've known each other since our freshman year of college, when we were thrown into a quad together."

"And tight ever since?"

"Very. But they didn't tell me they hated him. If I'd have known, I probably would've ignored it, but still. We were never meant to be a couple and should've split back then, but I didn't know how to leave him."

"You work with kids in situations like that."

"I do, but I didn't have that kind of training yet—and didn't see the forest for the trees."

Alan nodded and finished his first piece of pizza. "I've been there. You think you get it, and you find out you're wrong. Sucks."

"What sucks is that it took me so long to figure it out. I fell hard for Gil. We dated for almost ten years and I finally told him that we needed to get married or split. That should've been a clue to me that he wasn't invested, but I pushed it. We married within a month. I wanted to adopt and he didn't. I wanted to move up at work and he expected that so I could bankroll his lifestyle."

"He liked to spend?"

"Boy did he," Bram said. "He hated when I spent money on Kay, but needed me to drop cash on him. We divorced three years ago and I'm still healing."

"It's hard," Alan said. "You think you're in love, but they aren't and you can't get over it. They move right on while you're stuck."

"My heart took a lot longer to heal, yes." Bram fiddled with his glass. "Part of me will always love him — not who he is now, but the person I thought he was. I had a dream that I'd found the guy I'd been looking for and he turned out to be someone else."

"It'll take time."

"I know. I need to find someone patient enough to handle my heart." Could Alan be that person?

"You deserve that."

"So do you."

"Where is Gil now?" Alan asked and finished his pizza. "Still around here?"

"He moves around a lot. One week he might be around and the next three months he'll go somewhere else. He can't settle down."

Alan snorted. "He wanted to be free?"

"He wanted to figure out who he is and where he needed to be. Truth is, he didn't like that I wasn't giving him a blank check to spend. He wanted to be the center of my attention and with a child, that's impossible."

"It is." Alan left his plate on the table. "Mine was angry all the time."

"I'm sorry." His heart broke. No one deserved to be treated poorly.

"Rae never wanted to settle down, either. According to him, I wasn't wealthy or handsome enough. I needed to play better or stop playing a little kid's game and keep a real job. When I taught, it wasn't good enough. He kicked my self-esteem all around.'

"I'm sure he did. Terrible." Bram ate his pizza. "I hate to admit it, but I'm kind of relieved I'm not the only one."

"You're not. Rae left me for a new man. The last I knew, he's not even with that guy. He's moved on a couple times since then," Alan said. "To be honest, I'm a bit shocked he didn't bring something home."

Bram nodded. "Yes. They do that, too. They do it and don't care. Like you don't matter, as long as they get what they want."

"Yes." Alan leaned back in his seat. "Is Kaysen okay with everything?"

"With us?"

"No, with Gil."

Bram abandoned his plate. "I take him to a counselor and he does an online program, too. I let him talk to the counselors and adapt as I'm told what's going on. We have long talks, too. I keep an eye on him and he tells me how he feels. He hates Gil."

"I can see why," Alan said. "Does he hate me now?"

"No. He's unsure of you because he wants to be certain you're here for me, not some other reason. He'll come around the longer we're together — if we manage it." He had no doubts.

"If his feelings change, then tell me." Alan finished his tea. "Do you need to spend time with him tonight? I can go."

He didn't understand. "You're so quick to want to leave. Did I do something wrong?"

"No. I don't want to step on his toes."

Bram picked up his plate. "He's fine. I'll bet he's asleep on the futon. He crashes so hard after one game. Now that he's had two, he's had pizza and soda and cheesy bread in his belly...he's probably passed out. Get another slice and I'll check on him, but don't go. I like talking to you."

"If you're sure." Alan stood. He walked with Bram to the kitchen.

"I'll check on him. Give me a second." Bram left Alan by the bar and ducked into the rec room behind the garage. As he'd expected, Kaysen was stretched out on the futon, his socks and undershirt off. He snored happily. He'd eaten three quarters of the pizza and most of his cheesy bread. The television screen was on the menu page, waiting for him to choose another video.

Bram switched off the television and dimmed the lights. He draped a thin blanket over Kayse and left the room.

When he returned to the kitchen, Alan stood by the island.

"Everything okay?" Alan filled his glass with more tea. "Sorry. I was thirsty."

"You're fine," Bram said. "He's out. He made it through most of his pizza, but his video is over and he's snoring. He does that when his allergies flare."

"Oh."

"He's got a grass allergy and was born with enlarged adenoids." Bram filled his glass with tea. "He loves being outside, but the pollen doesn't like him."

"That's terrible." Alan sank onto one of the stools. "Why didn't you decide to follow your talents into professional baseball?"

"Easy." Bram sat beside him. "I didn't have the drive to stay that competitive. I love the game, but I wanted to teach."

"History, right?"

"You remembered." Bram grinned. He liked men who paid attention.

"I did." Alan held his glass in both hands. "I wanted to teach math and history, but I went for physical education instead. I liked gym and wanted kids to love it, too."

"Kaysen loves it, but he hates the state tests."

"They're not for everyone."

"Why'd you stop teaching?" Bram asked. He could talk to Alan about anything.

"I didn't want to keep playing endless games of dodgeball because the school system I was in wanted to get rid of the specials. I figured, why should I put effort in when I won't get to keep my job?"

"I hate when we have to get rid of programs because of money. We end up having to bring them back because we need them." Bram shook his head. "I'm sorry that happened."

"I am, too. I quit before the system fired me. I hated it, but whatever. I got the job at the sports center and that helped. It let me stay with the sports I love. I work with kids who want to play and work on their skills, so that's another good thing."

"At least you got a prime deal after. Have you ever considered coming back to teaching?"

"No. I'd need the perfect reason to come back and I don't have one."

"Maybe you'll find one."

"Maybe." Alan swept his gaze over Bram. "I hate to admit I'm not good at dating. I feel so silly right now."

"Why?" He didn't. The more Alan looked at him, the more he swore the temperatures in the room spiked.

"I don't know what to do," Alan murmured.

"How so?"

"Part of me wants to kiss you. I've wanted to since we worked in the stand. That's gotta be strange, right? We barely know each other." Alan balled his hands on the bar.

Trying to keep from reaching for him? "Is it taking all of your concentration to keep your hands to yourself?" Bram asked.

"Yes." Alan flattened his hands. "I feel like a clumsy teen. I want to make a move, but I'm nervous."

"Me, too." He'd never felt like this before. Like he knew what he wanted to do, but had no idea how to do it.

"Yes." Alan leaned into him and rested his forehead on Bram's. "I haven't been kissed in four years."

"No?" He smoothed his hand over Alan's thigh. Christ. He swore touching Alan scorched him from within. He needed more. Alan's breath tickled his face. Was his heart racing, too?

"Bram?" Alan asked.

"Want me to back off?" He needed to know.

"No."

"Then what?"

"Kiss me." Alan inched closer and feathered his mouth over Bram's.

Bram groaned into the kiss. He dug his nails into Alan's thigh. He wanted Alan closer. Like on his lap. He'd felt this way before, this rush, but Alan made the feelings fresh. Like it never should end.

He brushed his nose along Alan's. He threaded his fingers into Alan's short hair. His thoughts scattered and he couldn't think straight.

Alan broke the kiss, but kept him close. "Bram?"

"Yeah?" All he saw right now was Alan.

"We need to stop."

"Why?" He saw no earthly reason to.

"Kaysen's watching."

Fuck.

Chapter Seven

Alan backed up and swore his entire body was on fire. Not just because of the kiss. That'd set something alight in him he'd thought was long burned out. But the true embarrassment was in being caught. For all he knew, Kaysen was annoyed.

"Kay." Bram cleared his throat. "I thought you were asleep. I just checked on you."

"I wanted a Coke." Kaysen put his plate and the empty pizza box in the trash. "Sorry I interrupted."

"No, you didn't." Bram scrambled off the stool. "Wait." He followed Kaysen out of the room.

Alan sighed and bowed his head. Every time something good happened, he made a move to screw it up.

He'd have to tell Bram they should work as a team to find someone for each other, not mess this up worse by falling for each other. Should. But he'd become attached to Bram.

He stood and picked up the paper plates. He cleaned up the mess, tossing the trash in the bin. He closed the second pizza box after condensing the food into the single box and put the food in the fridge.

"What are you doing?"

Alan shoved the box onto the tray. "Cleaning up."

Bram clasped his hands together. "You're my guest. You don't have to. I should be doing that."

"You were busy, and it's time to clean up. I really should go." Alan tossed his napkin in the trash. "It's late." He walked across the kitchen to his shoes in the mud room.

"It's only quarter 'til eight."

"But you need time with your son." Why wasn't Bram understanding? "I'm in the way."

"Stop." Bram stood in the way. "May I speak?"

"Sure." He still wanted to get the hell out of there. He didn't belong here. He might like Bram, and he adored Kaysen, but he felt like the odd man out. He stepped into his sneakers. "I'm listening."

"Are you?" Bram remained in his way. "Please."

"I'm not one of your students." He wanted to sidestep out of Bram's path.

"No, you're not," Bram replied. "Kaysen isn't upset. I know you think he is, but he's not."

"No? He shot daggers at me when he looked at me." He refused to shout. "He didn't seem pleased."

"He's surprised."

"I know. This was a lot to throw at a kid." Alan sighed. "I didn't think. Can we go outside? I don't want to upset him more."

"Sure," Bram replied. "I didn't think either."

Megan Slayer

He waited until they were outside in the garage. "Then let's call it a hot experiment and move on. You don't want me as a complication."

"Who says I don't?" Bram asked. "Will you finally listen to me?"

"About what?" He strode to the open garage door to the fresh air of the early evening.

Bram stepped in front of him. "Kay's not mad. Yes, he's shocked, but he encouraged us to get together. He said he's okay with you. As long as you don't try to be a coach here at the house, he's fine."

That didn't seem right. He bowed his head and rested his hands on his hips.

"I know. Things went rather fast, but he's fine with us," Bram said. "I understand you want to go. I would want to as well. But I would like the chance to keep seeing you. Do you want to see me?" He kept his voice low.

"Bram." He didn't like being in this position.

"I have an end-of-the-year picnic and I need a date. Would you accompany me?" Bram asked.

"You really want me?" For a public date? It was so unreal. He needed to compose himself, but he did want to be seen with Bram.

"Yes. Would you go with me?"

He should think about it. Should really mull it over, weigh the pros and cons, consider everything. But his heart was involved. "Sure."

"Sure?"

"Yes." He might regret it, but oh well. He liked Bram.

"I'd like to try an actual date. If you don't want to, then tell me," Bram said.

Alan tipped his head and looked at Bram. "You're trying too hard. Yes, I'll go out with you. I have some doubts, but you're winning me over. Okay?" He had lots of worries about the relationship, but he'd give it all a go.

"What worries you?"

Where was he supposed to start? "Kaysen will end up hating me. Your ex will come back and the spark won't be gone, so you'll go back to him. You're a principal and I'm a coach. You'll realize you're gorgeous and can do better."

Bram sighed and rubbed Alan's arms. "Even if he does come back, I'm not interested. Gil did a lot of damage. I don't care what your job is. What I care about is that we mesh. I think we do."

"As for Kaysen? He's your priority. If you feel he's not happy because of me, then say so. I'll take my leave."

Bram balled his hands. "I will, but I don't foresee it."

"They never do," Alan muttered.

"What?"

"We have the potential for good things, but there are lots of things stacked against us. I won't get my hopes up for a while."

"Alan."

"Call it my guarded nature, but I already know the count and it's even right now, but can go south real fast."

"I'm sorry you've been hurt. I get how you feel and I'd like to try to heal together."

"Then let's give it a go." Alan hesitated. "I should go home. You need time with Kaysen and we should go a little slower."

"Can I call you?"

Bram folded his arms and widened his stance, but grinned. "I'm looking forward to it."

"I am, too."

Bram inched closer. "I felt the earth shift when you kissed me. Felt brand new, too. Haven't had that happen ever. Not with Gil. Not until you."

"You're too nice." He remained close to Bram. "I like you and I want to see you again. I'll text you, but we need to slow down. If we go too fast, it'll make us flame out. I don't want that."

Bram toyed with the front of Alan's shirt, like he needed the time to figure out what to say. "Okay."

"Okay?"

"Yeah. I'm trying to force things to happen faster because I'm nervous that it won't happen, but it will when it's supposed to."

"Exactly." He rested his hand on Bram's hip. He did like touching Bram. "I want to rush, too, but I don't want to ruin it before we get the chance to have it. Nor come between you and your son."

"You won't."

"I'll call you later. Spend time with Kay. He's looking forward to it." He kissed Bram once more, and didn't want to stop, but did. "Thanks for inviting me over. I had a great time."

"So did I." Bram let go and waved. "I look forward to your call."

"Me, too." He forced himself to his truck and ended up behind the wheel. Although he wanted to stay with Bram and let nature take its course, he drove home. He needed a shower and to stretch out. He could use a few minutes in the shower to take care of his erection he'd tried to hide, too.

It was too soon to be having those feelings for Bram, but he did. He'd fallen for Bram. The connection was strong.

He drove across town to his condo. It wasn't the most exciting place to live, but it was enough. He parked in the carport next to his unit, then locked the vehicle. He made his way inside and closed the door. Once he kicked out of his shoes, he froze.

Was that his doorbell?

How? He'd just been outside and hadn't seen anyone.

He checked the peephole. Sure enough, there was someone on the stoop.

He engaged the chain, then opened the door. "Rae."

"Hi, baby." Rae twisted the knob. "Let me in. I miss you."

"Miss me?" He almost laughed. "You walked out on me."

"I was wrong. Open the door and let me in. I made a mistake."

"Which time?" Alan asked. "The first time you cheated on me? The second? Third? You lied to me and exposed me to so much. Now you want to come back?"

"You always make it sound so much worse than it is. Stop being dramatic."

"Me?" He tended to talk too much in moments like this. He hated silence, yet Rae had rendered him speechless.

"Yes, you. This is what you do. You spin the story so it's about you and how you've been hurt. You're the one who broke it off with me. You broke my heart. Now I hear you moved on. You told me I could always come home, but you lied about that, too. You lie about everything."

He refused to listen to this any longer. He knew the script. Rae would yell, he'd gaslight. He'd blame, then he'd get violent. "Sorry."

"Sorry. Yeah, you'd better be sorry, you worthless sack of shit. What would your fancy principal do if he found out you're a whore?"

He should've never let that stupid restraining order lapse in the first place. He slammed the door shut and flipped the deadbolt into place. He darted into the kitchen, the room furthest from the door and hid behind the cabinets. He withdrew his cell from his pocket. Time to call the police.

"Nine-one-one, what's the nature of your emergency?"

His voice wavered and his hands trembled as he sank to the floor. "My ex-boyfriend is outside my condo and he's threatening me." He winced at the pounding on the door.

"Where are you? Are you in a safe place?" the dispatcher asked.

"I'm hiding in the corner of the kitchen. I'm at fourteen Hopper Court." He curled down tight. "This isn't my first time calling." He'd had a restraining order against Rae before, but let it expire when he thought Rae had moved out of state. He never should've let it end.

"We have a unit on the way. Stay where you are and don't engage. Does your ex have a gun?"

Jesus. He had no idea. "I don't know. I can't see him." He trembled. "He will tell the police this is my fault."

"You'll be okay. Just stay where you are and stay on the line. The police should be there soon."

"I see the lights." The blinking blue and red lit up the condo. He hated being scared. Hated having to worry if he'd get hurt. He didn't care if his truck was attacked or if there was damage to the condo. What he did care about was not being killed.

A pounding on the door interrupted his thoughts.

"That should be the police," the dispatcher said. "Check."

He peeked around the corner, then inched over to the door. He checked the peephole. Sure enough, there were two officers. "I see them. Thanks." He hung up, tucked the phone in his back pocket before answering the door.

"Hello, we'd like a word with you," the taller officer said. "I'm Officer Greene."

He recognized the officers, Greene and Monroe. They'd responded the last time. "Yes, officers."

"He's in the back of Greene's car. What happened tonight?" Monroe asked.

He gave a full recounting of the day, including the run-in with Rae. "I didn't encourage him."

"Are you parading the new relationship?" Greene asked. "Where he feels intimidated?"

"No. It's not even much of anything. We just decided to try something today."

"Understood." Monroe spoke into his radio. "Yes, we will."

Greene stood between Alan and the squad car. "I'm sorry he keeps coming around. I'd file a restraining order again to keep him away. He claims he's got his name on the condo. Is that true?"

"No. This one is in my name." He'd go to the police department tonight to get this straightened out. This had to end.

"He's destroyed your fenders and tailgate. We know because we watched. He also punched your mailbox, so we're taking him in tonight to cool down," Monroe said. "We have him on destruction of property. Come in and file that restraining order."

"I will, but I can't hide from him. I'm a coach. I work with the school. I can't abandon my team because he wants to be destructive."

"I heard you made the play-offs. First team to do that in twenty years at the junior high level," Greene said. "Congrats."

"The team is the reason I won't hide," Alan replied. "Thanks."

"You're safe right now. I'd get that order and try to stay away from him," Monroe said.

"I will." He waited until the police left before he took photos of the damage to the truck. He groaned. This was the second vehicle he'd had to replace because of Rae's destruction.

He debated trying to use the truck or getting a rideshare to go to the police department. He'd leave the truck in case Rae had stuffed something in it or up the tailpipe. *Rideshare it is.*

While he waited for the driver, he texted Bram.

Sorry. Will be late to call you. My ex showed up.

Within a few seconds, a reply came.

What happened? Are you all right?

He sighed.

I'm fine. He bashed my truck and mailbox. I'm going to the police department to file a restraining order.

He hit send then wrote a second text.

No hard feelings if you decide you don't want to see me.

He had to give Bram the out. Had to explain to him why this might not be a great situation. Most guys would see the mess Alan was in and run. Hell, he might run himself.

And Bram had a kid to think about. He had bigger issues.

I'm worried about you, came the reply.

He shook his head. Tears burned at the corners of his eyes. He had to answer Bram, but he didn't want to.

I'm fine. I've been through worse.

Rae had done so much worse and kept going. This was no different. He'd been dangerous and Alan had to figure out how to sort it out after.

His phone rang. He expected it to be his rideshare, but instead, it was Bram.

"Hi." He wasn't really in the mood to talk to anyone, but secretly, he appreciated someone cared.

"What happened?" Bram asked.

"My ex came over, he found out I had a date, he believes I'm in a relationship and he wanted back. When I said no, he flipped. I called the police and they took him away for the night."

"He destroyed your truck?"

"He smashed the fenders and tailgate, but it's dark enough I can't tell the full level of destruction. It'll be okay."

"No."

"Bram."

"How are you getting to the PD? On foot?"

"No, I called a rideshare. I should hear from him soon." He hoped. Where was the driver? He should check the app.

"Can you call it off? I'm coming to get you."

"Bram." He didn't like being pushed around. "You don't have to take full control."

"I know I don't, but I called my mother. She's going to be here in ten minutes to stay with Kaysen. I'll take you to the PD."

"Bram." This was going too far.

"I insist, because I want to be sure my friend is safe."

His friend. It was something.

"Alan, I like you and I'd like to keep seeing you, but I want to protect you first."

"You don't understand what I've been through, or what I'm up against."

"No, I don't, but that's no reason to give up on you. When you care about someone, even if it is new, you don't quit on them. You're my friend and my son's coach, so I care."

He pinched the bridge of his nose. He wasn't going to argue any longer because he doubted he'd make a dent, even if he tried. "I need to see where the rideshare is at, but I can cancel it." Truth be told, he did want a friend to go with him to the police department. He'd gone the first time on his own and it'd been both liberating and scary as fuck.

He checked the app and realized he'd never actually ordered the damn rideshare. *Fuck.* He bowed his head.

"Mom's here, so I'm leaving and putting you on the Bluetooth on the car. I'll be there in ten minutes. You're on Hopper?"

"Yes, I'm outside the condo on my stoop. You'll see me." There was no chance to miss him. His self-esteem and energy were gone. Every time Rae showed up, he sapped everything from the situation. Rae wore him out.

"I'm on my way," Bram said. "Talk to me."

He sank onto the stoop. He hung his head and rubbed his temples. "I don't need to be saved."

"No, but you don't need to be alone. This is a garbage situation."

"Bram." He needed a second. "What about you and your son? What about your mother? They need you."

"Alan."

He wasn't getting through. "We live in a small town. The same grapevine that led my ex back here to find out if I had a boyfriend is the same one who could ruin you because of me."

"I disagree."

Bram would drive him crazy.

"I'm not worried about my reputation because I worked hard for it. If someone doesn't like me after one episode, then they didn't from the first. I won't be able to change their mind and I don't want to. I'm good where I am, and if that's with you, then even better. I'm halfway there. Shouldn't be another minute or two."

He didn't know what to say. Nothing would disarm Bram.

"I see you." With that, Bram hung up. He pulled up in front of the condo and parked at the end of the short drive.

Alan's knees buckled. Thank God he was sitting. He hadn't changed his clothes, taken a shower or given himself time to process. He bowed his head. "Hi."

Bram left his car door open and rushed up to Alan. "You're okay?"

"Yeah."

"Get in the car. I'm going to film your truck and the mailbox. You need it to be documented for posterity. I'll even added a timestamp to them, too."

He wanted to say something, but didn't. He doubted anything short of a force of nature would stop Bram. He checked he'd locked the condo and wandered over to the car. He sank onto the passenger seat.

A few moments later, Bram joined him in the car. "I used my flashlight to film it. He bashed the hell out of your truck."

"He did."

"But, it can be saved — if he didn't sugar the gas tank or stuff something in the tailpipe."

"How?" He wanted to hide. There wasn't enough time to do those things, but still. It didn't matter.

"The joint vocational school has an entire program to rehab vehicles and they'd love to get a hold of the truck. They'd do it for cost, if even that, because they're getting the experience."

"Yeah." He'd worry about the truck later. Right now, he didn't care.

"Alan."

"I'm tired."

"I'll bet."

"You don't get it." He paused. Maybe Bram did. "My ex crops up when I think I've got my life sorted out. He comes along to destroy what I've built and usually succeeds. I'm tired of rebuilding. I'm tired of having to keep an eye out. Jesus. I'm just plain fucking tired."

Coaching Love

"I do understand. Gil does something similar. He doesn't get violent, but he's more emotional. He saps the energy from everything."

He closed his eyes. "I'm sorry."

"Why?"

"Because people can't be normal to each other. They have to be crabby and angry. Listen to me. I'm being crabby and angry. I'm swearing and I don't like to."

"You're hurt and he's been mean."

"Yes. And what does that anger and meanness get anyway? Broken stuff and trashed hearts. It's not right."

"No, it's not."

"And we've got to pick up the pieces."

"We do." Bram left the driveway. "We'll come back here when we're done."

"We? Don't you need to get home to Kaysen?"

"When I told Mom what I needed, she was thrilled to help. She loves spending time with Kay and was hurt that she couldn't make it to his game, but she had to work today."

"Oh." He tried to lift himself out of his funk. "Where does she work?"

"She's a librarian in Avon and they were open today, which meant she was there all day. She lives five minutes away, so it wasn't a big deal to drive over. Hell, I think she was hoping I'd call," Bram said. "She also rather liked that I have someone I'm worried about, so she wanted to help. She's also happy I'm not fretting over Gil."

He nodded and tried to compose himself. "I'm seriously tired. I'm tired of fighting with him."

"You don't have to fight alone."

110

"No, but I don't want him to lash out at you or Kaysen. I'd never be able to live with myself if something happened to Kaysen." He didn't want them to get hurt. "It's a small town and people talk."

"They do, but you need to understand I have that under control. Kaysen is way more aware than even I knew. He's guarded because of Gil and won't let your ex get close to him." Bram parked in front of the police department. "I'll go in with you."

"Thanks." He sighed and forced himself to focus on what he had to do. He'd done this before and wasn't a fan of going through it again. But here he was. "I hate this."

"Being at the police department?"

"Getting a damn restraining order." He shook his head. "Just leave each other alone, you know? You've split up. If you can't be cordial, then don't even bother each other."

"I get it." Bram left the car and locked it as Alan stood on the sidewalk. "He's in here?"

"Supposed to be." He stuffed his hands into his pockets. "I'm shocked it's not all around town. I bet they know I'm coming in because it's made it through the grapevine."

"Oh, probably." Bram held the door for him. "And probably that I'm here."

"I know..." He needed to stop that.

Bram held up his hand. "I don't care. Let them talk."

He gritted his teeth. This still wasn't worth trashing Bram's reputation. He wandered into the police department to the main desk.

The officer looked up. "I've been expecting you."

"You have?" He knew they would. "And why?"

"A restraining order." The officer got the paperwork out. "He's back there complaining and crying."

"Crying." Good Lord. Rae could be so dramatic. "I'm sorry."

"Monroe and Greene also let me know you were coming in. Your...friend keeps saying you're coming in to ruin his reputation." The officer half-shrugged. "Let's get this filled out."

Alan answered the questions as best he could, giving as much detail as possible. Having Bram there both helped and embarrassed him. He never should've gotten in this deep with Rae.

"I'll get this to the judge and we'll be set." The officer tapped the papers on the desk. "Did they get your statement?"

"At the scene? Yes." He stuffed his ID back into his wallet. "That takes effect immediately, right?"

"It does," the officer replied. "It's not fun filling these out, but I'd rather you be protected."

"Agreed," Bram said.

"Mr. Rode, how are you?" the officer asked. "I saw you but I wanted to get this done first. How's Kay?"

"He pitched and got the win today," Bram said. "How'd Jona do? She had a meet today, didn't she?"

"She took first on the beam, then second in her swim meet in the butterfly." The officer grinned. "She's finally finding what makes her happy."

"Good," Bram said. "That's what matters."

Alan agreed. In an odd way, he appreciated not having to talk. He didn't mind being invisible. It gave him time to think.

"Good game today, Coach," another officer said. "Those boys will win it all."

"I have faith," Alan replied. He didn't mind talking about baseball, but he wanted to go home. He'd had enough, but would home be safe? It would be tonight, but probably not tomorrow. He could sleep in his office at the club. *Shit.* He needed a ride. "Will my truck be impounded?"

"Yes." Bram offered his phone. "I documented the damage to the truck and the mailbox. I have the file here."

Officer Greene rounded the desk. "Thanks. We will add it to the file. And yes, it's a crime scene, so we would appreciate it if you leave the vehicle for further documentation."

"Sure." He had to sort this all out. Somehow.

"We all get involved with people we wish we hadn't," Officer Greene said. "And it's a small town, so everyone knows your business. It sucks, yet it doesn't. People do look out for each other, and for you, this way."

"Sure." It didn't feel like it.

"You're free to go. Try to get some rest," the first officer said.

"Yeah." Alan wanted to hide deep in a hole.

"I'll make sure he does," Bram said. "And I don't care who knows." He slipped his arm around Alan and led him out of the police department.

He leaned into Bram, thankful for the support. "You're too nice to me."

"Nah." Bram opened the car door. "You're a friend and in a rough spot. Of course I'll help. I'd like to be with you and take care of you, so that doesn't hurt."

"You would?" He'd heard what Bram said, but he hardly believed it.

"I would, and I'm insisting you get a bag and bring it to the house. You can crash in my room."

"What about you? I can't sleep in your bed." Not that he didn't want to. "Not with your mom and kid there." That wouldn't be right.

"My mom's in the guest room, Kaysen is in his room and you can have the bed in my office. It's connected to my room, so you won't be seen if you don't want to be, and can get a shower in peace."

It sounded too good to be true. "Bram."

"I insist. It's almost Sunday, we have nowhere to go and should have a do-nothing day," Bram said. "You deserve it."

"I have to call in at the club." Not until noon, but still.

"So you do. Call in and rest. I insist." A wicked gleam filled Bram's eyes. "I won't let you go until you've had a decent night's sleep."

"You won't let up until I agree, will you?" Alan asked. He should've known. Bram knew how to handle tough situations. While he struck Alan as pushy, Bram also seemed to understand how to take care of things. How to be kind while being firm.

He couldn't resist Bram.

"I won't let up until I know you're safe and sound," Bram said.

Alan gave up. He didn't feel like fighting. He'd rather rest, and if he could with Bram, then fine.

"Well?" Bram asked.

"Let's go. I have a date with your couch—and you."

Bram grinned. "It's not how I envisioned spending the night with you, but it's perfect."

Bram could put a positive spin on anything. "It is."

He wasn't sure what he'd gotten into, but it was too late to turn back. "Then let's go."

It was his shot at forever.

Time to take it.

Chapter Eight

Bram waited outside the condo and kept a watch. When Alan had insisted on going in alone, he hadn't put up a fight, but he'd wanted to. He also wanted Alan to feel secure. Right now, he felt helpless. He kept watching in case Rae came back. There was no chance it'd happen if Rae was locked up all night to cool off, but that didn't matter.

His phone buzzed. *Damn it.* He didn't want to talk to anyone. He should be vigilant, but it could be his son.

The phone buzzed again. He groaned as he checked the screen. Tim. He sent his friend a quick text.

Will chat with you later. Had stuff come up.

Where was Alan? What was taking him so long?

He opened the car door. "Alan?"

"Sorry." Alan stepped out of the condo and locked the door. "I couldn't decide what to take and what to leave. I don't want to leave anything that's worth something in case Rae comes back when he's released. He's spiraling."

"Do you have a safe?"

"Locked. It's heavy, but if he can lift it, he'll end up hurting." Alan tugged on the door. "Let's go. I need a break."

"You do." He climbed back into the driver's side of the car. "Can I ask how you met Rae?"

"May."

"You met in May?" He put the car in reverse.

"No." Alan fastened his seatbelt. "May you ask."

"Oh." He laughed at his mistake. "I did ask that incorrectly."

"And you're the principal."

"I know, right?" Bram backed down the short drive. "I'm human."

"You are." Alan stretched his legs. "I need to contact someone from the vocational school about the truck."

"We'll have to worry about it on Monday. I know who to talk to, but they don't answer their phone on Sundays."

"Sure," Alan replied. "And, yes, you may ask about Rae. There isn't much to tell. We met at a club. He approached first and I thought he was cute and single."

He drove away from the condo and flexed his hands on the wheel. "He wasn't?"

"Nope. He had a boyfriend at the time and didn't tell me. He kept it quiet until we were involved for a month."

The asshole. "How'd you find out?"

"The guy showed up at the house I was renting and was pissed, hurt and wanted to eviscerate me. I apologized because I had no idea," Alan said. "I felt so dumb, but I was in his web. I fell for it when he said he'd broken things off with the guy. They were still in the process of falling apart. Poor guy."

"Was his name Guy?"

"Actually, it was. I pronounced it Gee like he was French and he wasn't, but he thought it was funny. We ended up becoming friends. When I see him, he's Gee."

"Well, at least you have that."

"It's about all I have," Alan said. "I dated Rae for three years and tried living with him for six months. My heart was more involved than his ever was. I moved four times for him and even helped him buy a car. This is how he repays me — he trashes my stuff."

Bram drove the long way around the neighborhood, afraid that once they got to the house, Alan would stop talking. "You seem to be okay, though. Or are you struggling more than you let on?"

"More than I let on. I try to keep it under wraps so no one knows."

"Not even your mom knows?"

"She'd love to know, but she died when I was seventeen. Dad disowned me when he found out I was gay."

"Ouch." He'd never had to have that discussion. His mother had been wonderful when he came out.

Alan snorted. "He's a womanizer and was a terrible parent, so I lucked out with him leaving me alone."

"When did you come out?"

"When I was thirteen. I knew early on that I was gay. I liked the way the trim ballplayers looked in their uniforms and lusted after them during the hot games. If they had their shirt off, then I was in." Alan laughed. "I was so horny."

"You're human too."

"I guess so."

He pulled into the driveway and into the empty garage. "Mom likes to park in the turnaround."

"It's handy and out of the way."

"It is."

"You don't have to put on a façade for me. If you're struggling, then tell me. Put on one for Mom and Kay, sure, but not me. I want to help you," Bram said and parked. He turned off the engine. "I'm here."

"I know you are."

He closed the big garage door, but stayed in the car. "Expect Mom to want to meet you. Kay has told her lots about his coach."

"Good things?"

"Always. Kaysen is a kid, but he's not a mean kid."

"Cool."

He paused. "I know you're a million miles away right now. I get it. You've been through too much in the last twenty-four hours. I'm not trying to get you into my bed, but I want you to rest. Crash in my office. No one will bother you and if you want to talk, then we'll talk. If you want to be quiet, then we'll do that. It's fine."

"I know."

He felt so helpless. All he wanted to do was give Alan comfort. Right now, he needed to give him space.

"No one's ever given me this kind of consideration. I usually have to muscle through, so forgive me if I'm a mess," Alan said. "I guess I've just known the wrong people."

"Now you know some of the right ones." He couldn't help himself as he tugged Alan close. He wrapped his arms around Alan, wanting to take away his pain.

Alan trembled, then made a sound that was a cross between a laugh and a cry.

"It's okay." He petted Alan's hair. "It'll be okay."

"I hate feeling like this. I hate being helpless."

"I know." He hated that Alan had been abused and hurt. "You're safe." Alan's strength amazed him. Most people would've crumbled by now, but Alan kept going. Unless someone knew his situation, Alan had hidden it well. He'd bet the players didn't know about Alan's struggle.

Alan sighed and pulled away. "I need to go inside. My head hurts and I stink."

"I hadn't noticed." He bit back a chuckle. "Let's go inside. I've got a back staircase if you'd rather use that than face the firing squad of my mother."

"Thanks." Alan stared at him. "I feel so silly. I'm forty-five years old and hiding from a bully. I teach the players to stare down bullies at the plate, but I'm not doing that. I'm sneaking up the steps and hiding from my bully and your family. What kind of example is that?"

"One who needs a break." He caressed the back of Alan's neck. "We live under a microscope and you need to heal in private. You can do that here."

"Thank you." Alan leaned into him. "You're a gem."

"So are you." He brushed his nose against Alan's and breathed in his scent. "Come on."

"Sure."

He left the car and waited for Alan before retrieving the bag from the backseat. He directed Alan into the house. The silence enveloped Bram. He didn't even hear the television.

"This way." Bram pointed to the back steps that led to his office. He switched on the light at the top of the stairs. "My room is through the main door. I've got plenty of stuff in the shower, so take your time. I'll get a couple more towels and pillows. That way you've got some space."

"Thanks."

He paused in the doorway leading to his room. "Will you promise me something?"

"What?" Alan dropped his bag. "Not to leave?"

"Please, don't go."

"I won't. I don't have any strength. You can check on me all you want. I'll be here."

"I'm holding you to that." He squeezed Alan's fingers, then left him alone to let his mother know they'd returned.

He found her in the guest room. She was sitting up in bed with a book and only the bedside light on. "You're in here already?" he asked.

"Within fifteen minutes of my arriving, Kaysen fell asleep. I had to walk him up the stairs to his room," Lindy said. "I got him to brush his teeth at least." She closed the book and tossed it aside.

"I'm not shocked. He played hard today."

"He found videos on social media of the game and showed me. We watched all that were available. He did play well and for a while, I saw a mini version of you on that field. He's so much like you at that age."

"Thanks, Mom."

"How's your friend? Alan?"

"Fragile." He sat on the end of the bed. "He's been through a lot. He feels fragile, but he's stronger than he thinks."

"It sounded like he's had too much to deal with," she said. "Did you consult the support group? Have they signed off on him?"

"I haven't told them about him yet." He glanced over his shoulder. "I'm a little afraid they'll overwhelm him."

"They might." Lindy fiddled with her book. "Is he okay? You sounded pretty concerned."

"His ex got pushy and he's a bully, but this was too much. Alan needs a place to be safe."

"And you'll keep my grandson safe?" she asked and stared at him. "Bramford?"

He hated when she used his full name. It made him feel like a child. He was forty-six years old. "Yes, Mom. I've kept him safe from Gil."

"You have," she said. "He visited the library."

His stomach churned. "No, no, no. Did he cause trouble?"

"No." She narrowed her eyes. "All I'm going to say is that I want to meet this one, and you'd better be careful. Gil's getting bolder, and if he sees that you've moved on, he might try to be stupid. He hates to lose."

"I know." He nodded, already planning how he'd protect Kaysen. "I'm on it."

"I never doubted that," Lindy said. "Just keep your eyes open."

"I will. You can stay here, Ma. Would that be better?"

"We can't hide forever. We can keep living our lives. That's what annoys him—we don't hide away and let him win."

"True." He'd keep his wits about him, but she was right—he needed to stop worrying and keep living.

"You like this guy? Is his name Alan?"

"Alan Klane. He's Kaysen's baseball coach. You've met him—last year when he played with the seventh-grade team. He's a good coach, and reminds me of many of mine when I played. He's very fair."

"Is he?" She grinned. "Or are you partial?"

"Both." She'd caught him. "Oh well."

She kept grinning and shook her head. "It's nice to see my old Bram back."

"Yeah?" He thought Alan brought out the best in him.

"Yes. You seem happier, and even though Gil is causing trouble, you're relaxed. I like seeing it."

"The last time I felt this way is when I played ball."

"I can see that. Go take care of him. I'm fine, and I'll stick around tomorrow so we can have a barbecue," she said. "We'll have fun."

"We will." He liked that idea. One big, happy family.

"Go take care of him. I'm turning in," she said. "I only stayed up to ensure you got home without incident."

"Thanks, Mom. See you in the morning." He stood and rapped his knuckles on the doorframe. "Good night."

"'Night, Bram."

He wandered down the hallway to his bedroom. Steam billowed from the bathroom. When he peeked into the adjacent room, he noticed Alan had left the bathroom door open. He spied Alan's bare ass in the shower. Was this intentional teasing?

His mouth watered and he bit back a groan. *Damn.* Alan was toned all over. He longed to wrap his arms around him. When Alan turned, Bram noticed a tattoo of a ball and bat on his hip. What a naughty surprise! He liked that Alan had a secret devilish side. He visually traced the faint line of dark hair from Alan's navel to his groin.

A gasp lodged in his throat when he saw Alan's cock. Long and thick, enough to please, but not monstrous. He'd bet Alan tasted good, too.

Something behind him buzzed. *Shit*. He'd forgotten about his phone. He didn't want to rip his gaze from Alan's naked body.

Still, he needed to answer. If the support group was on the other end of the text, then they'd keep texting until they got a reply.

He returned to the bedroom and picked up the phone. Sure enough, Tim had texted three times. He groaned as the phone rang. He answered, "Hi."

"You ignored me. You're talking to me now, so either he's a terrible lay or you're alone. What gives?" Tim asked.

"What gives is that he's showering and in the other room. He's a good guy. I don't know if he's a good or bad lay — we haven't slept together."

Tim clicked his tongue. "You dog. You found someone. Really?"

"I did."

"I need details."

"I don't have time." He glanced over his shoulder. The steam dissipated and he didn't hear the shower. "He's here and I'll fill you in tomorrow or Monday. Okay? I won't not tell you."

"You'd better, and expect we're all chewing this over."

"I did, but don't you all have lives?" He knew the truth. They loved to gossip.

"We love you and we worry."

"I need to go." He wanted to help Alan. Maybe after some comfort, he'd have a chance to talk to the support group. "I'll talk to you later."

"Okay, but I will annoy you if you don't," Tim said, then hung up.

He scrubbed the back of his hand across his forehead. He loved the support group as if they were his real brothers, but like family, they drove him nuts.

"You didn't have to hang up on my account," Alan said. "You don't have to adjust for me."

He tensed, then faced Alan. Alan stood in the doorway of the bathroom and wore nothing but a towel around his narrow waist. He rested his hands on his hips and water dripped from his hair.

"I'm fine," Alan said. "I can handle myself."

"You can." He abandoned his phone on the bed and crossed the room to Alan. "I— Wow."

Alan rocked on the balls of his feet. "You look like you could eat me."

"I'd like to." He had to keep himself in check. "You're dangerous. No one should be that sexy."

Alan blushed. "Everyone looks hot right out of the shower. Wait until I'm all sweaty and then make a call."

He groaned. He'd seen that, too and liked it. "You passed my muster."

"I did?" Alan's blush deepened.

"I did." He shouldn't push this, but he needed to touch Alan. Blood rushed to his dick and he swore he felt his pulse throughout his body. His breath lodged in his throat. "Noticed everything about you."

"Bram."

He splayed his hand on Alan's chest. The heat seeped into his own body. He raked his nails over Alan's pec. "May I?"

"What?"

"Kiss you?" He vibrated with need. "Can't push you, but I can't hold back, either." But he'd follow Alan's cues.

"Kiss me." Alan bridged the gap between them and feathered his mouth over Bram's. He pressed his body to Bram's and the bulge beneath his towel pulsed against Bram's groin.

Bram threaded his arms around Alan and held him closer. He grinded on Alan. *Holy hell.* Alan was addicting. He opened to Alan and when Alan matched his moves, he sucked on Alan's tongue. Raw need spiraled through Bram's veins.

Alan walked him backward to the bed. Bram braced himself against the mattress. "Do you want this?" Bram asked. "I'll stop."

"No. I need this. Need you." Alan rested his forehead on Bram's.

"Let me close the door." Bram let go long enough to shut the door and when he turned, Alan had settled on the bed. The towel parted, giving Bram a glimpse of his tattoo.

Bram struggled with his shirt. He'd showered quickly earlier, after Alan had headed home, but he swore the temperature in the room spiked and he was flushed all over. He yanked his shirt over his head, then tossed the garment onto the floor.

"Wow." Alan sat up. The towel loosened and pooled around him, but he didn't seem to notice. He parted his lips. "My God."

"What?" He popped the button on his jeans. He inched up to Alan. "I'm not exciting."

"No?" Alan scooted to the edge of the bed and parted his legs. He reached for Bram.

When Bram situated himself between Alan's thighs, Alan pressed kisses to Bram's abdomen. His breath warmed Bram's skin.

Bram swore he tingled all over. He palmed Alan's head, needing to keep him close.

"Alan." Bram rocked into him. "You're so addicting. Don't want to stop."

"Then don't," Alan said between kisses. He hooked his fingers into Bram's jeans and tugged the denim down his legs.

Bram wriggled, encouraging the jeans to land at his feet. He tipped Alan's head back, forcing Alan to look him in the eye. "Want to taste you."

"Yes." Alan leaned back, stretching out on the mattress. His cock bobbed. Pre-cum glistened on the tip.

Bram licked his lips and shoved his briefs down to the floor. He kicked out of the bunched-up clothing, then knelt at the edge of the bed. He met Alan's gaze before he flicked his tongue across the blunt head of Alan's shaft. The salty taste of pre-cum exploded on his tongue. When Alan groaned, he encouraged Bram. He fisted his hands in the bedding. "Yes."

Bram refused to let Alan down. He opened his mouth and swallowed Alan to the back of his throat. He bobbed his head, creating a quick cadence in seconds.

Alan forked his fingers into Bram's hair. "You'll kill me."

He hoped not. He wanted to make Alan happy. He increased his pace, bobbing faster. Each time Alan bumped the back of his throat, Alan spurred him on. He groaned around Alan's shaft.

"Bram." Alan tensed. "My..." He didn't finish speaking. Instead, another groan filled the air.

Bram cupped Alan's balls in his fingers. He toyed with him, loving the feel of him in his hand. He caressed the skin behind Alan's hole while he pumped his mouth on Alan's dick.

"Oh, Jesus." Alan mashed his dick between Bram's lips. "Can't hold back."

He wasn't sure he wanted Alan to hold back *anything*. He needed Alan to come apart. He eased his index finger back to Alan's hole. Without penetrating him, Bram teased the sensitive skin of Alan's ass.

"Oh my Jesus." Alan tensed. He pulled hard on Bram's hair and surged deep into Bram's mouth. He growled, but said nothing intelligible.

As he surged forward, he came hard in Bram. Hot seed shot down Bram's throat.

Bram kept bobbing his head. He didn't want to miss a thing. He lapped at Alan. The man tasted so good, like wine.

Alan let go of Bram's hair and sank backward onto the bed. He slumped on the mattress. He panted and barely moved.

Bram added a few more licks before he withdrew with a pop. He then sat back on his heels. "Relaxed?"

"Yes," Alan managed. "Can't think straight."

"Then I did my job." He pressed his lips together, contented. "I liked pleasing you."

"You did." Alan covered his face with his arms. "I'm worn out."

"I'm sure." He stretched out nude beside Alan. "You're beautiful."

"So are you." Alan moved one arm and patted Bram's hip. "Everything in my brain says what we're doing is so bad, but I can't tell why."

"Because you're afraid to let yourself have something good. You think you don't deserve it." Bram slid his arm across Alan's taut belly. "You do deserve it."

"I do?" Alan met his gaze. "Why are you so nice to me? You barely know me."

He half-shrugged. "I can't explain it. I'm drawn to you, and see a kindred spirit in you. I enjoy your company, and you're very hot in the sack."

Alan furrowed his brow, but smiled. "I am?"

"Got me all hot and bothered."

"You got me off," Alan said. "I owe you."

"When you're ready." Bram curled up next to him. "You have no idea how handsome you are, how sweet and sensitive, how kind. You just see what your ex wants you to see. I know the truth."

Alan grinned, but his eyes were half-closed. He sighed. "I'm glad you see it."

"I won't let you forget it." He'd work every day to prove Alan's worth. "Rest. I'll stay here with you. Not sure I want to go."

"It's your room," Alan said. He didn't move. "You don't need to go. I should."

"Not when I'm enjoying holding you." He tucked Alan in closer. "Might even sleep better with you here."

"I want to argue with you, but I'm too worn out and you feel good, too. I want to stay here."

"Then do it." He yanked a blanket over them and managed to turn off the light. "I've been waiting for someone like you for so long. Maybe I've been waiting for you. Either way, I found you and I want to keep exploring."

"We have a few subjects in common," Alan murmured.

"Subjects?"

"Chemistry, biology, LGBTQ studies, bodily geometry..."

Now he understood. "Sports and education, too."

"We do. Good night." Alan closed his eyes and within seconds, began to snore lightly. He rolled onto his side and pressed his back against Bram's stomach.

Bram enjoyed the closeness. He caressed the tattoo on Alan's hip. He memorized every second of this time with him.

His thoughts wandered, though. He considered what Tim had said and his mother insinuated. He had jumped in with Alan rather quickly. That's how he tended to operate when it came to major decisions. Jump in and deal with the fallout later.

Most of the time, things worked out — like his return to Lakewood, with his current job and his adoption of Kaysen. The relationship with Gil was the exception to the rule. He snorted to himself. Was he replaying the situation with Gil?

No. Gil had been jealous of him. He detected no jealousy in Alan. Gil had wanted to *be* him. Not Alan. He'd had a baseball career all on his own. Alan was sweet and needed help, but could handle things by himself. Gil was all confidence and no remorse. Alan was empathetic.

No, this wasn't a replay of his time with Gil. This was better. He regretted nothing.

Bram's phone buzzed. *God damn it.* He let go of Alan long enough to silence the device. Who wanted him at this time of night? Whoever it was, they could wait.

The screen lit up again. He was tangled up with Alan, but checked the message.

He didn't recognize the number. Should he open the message? He read the preview without opening the text.

Saw the game. Our boy did well.

His stomach lurched. The number wasn't one he knew, but the message sounded like something Gill would say when trying to be kind, despite sounding fake. Somehow, Gil had found a way to weasel back in.

A moment later, the screen lit with another message.

You've moved on. He's cute.

No. He refused to do this again. He blocked the number. If Gil wanted to talk, he could talk to someone else. His attention was occupied.

Bram abandoned the device on the bed and cuddled up to Alan. He'd found his heart and wanted to see where the relationship took them. He couldn't do that with his attention divided.

Besides, Gil had his chance and squandered it. Now, it was Alan's turn.

Although he should sleep, he picked up the phone and sent the support group a text.

Had a kind of date tonight. Was good. He's a coach, plays baseball, is cute and even Kay likes him. Not Gil. I'm happy.

He hit send and waited for the replies. Hopefully, everyone was in bed and wouldn't get the text yet. Or maybe he wanted them to see it and know not to worry about him.

Tim replied first.

Go you. Sex him up.

Then Dante.

You need me to check him out? Can do a background check. Say the word and I will.

Josef answered last.

He's fine and happy. Let's give him a day to enjoy himself, then we pounce. We will pounce, Bram. Enjoy.

Ah, he loved his friends. They'd check on him, even if it drove him crazy. Good thing they all got along.

He put his phone back on silent and abandoned it on the nightstand. Within a few minutes, he fell asleep. For once, he collapsed with no help from melatonin or even sheer exhaustion. He had a sexy man in his bed and that was enough. He had the chance at stability, too.

Why not take this ride and see where it led?

He saw no reason to stop.

Maybe ever.

Chapter Nine

Alan woke to sunlight in the room and a warm body beside him. He glanced over at Bram. A grin pulled at the corners of his mouth. Yes, his life was out of control. His ex was causing issues, but he'd found a wonderful man to help him navigate the problems.

Bram was more than he'd ever imagined. For one, Bram cared. He'd come out when he didn't have to and had lent a hand. Second, he threw his heart into what he did. He might genuinely have feelings for Alan. Most of all, he was so sexy inside and out. The way his eyes sparkled and now he smiled...it was all too much.

How had he gotten so lucky to find Bram?

He stared at Bram. He was handsome, even in sleep.

Bram stretched, but didn't open his eyes. "You're staring at me."

"I am," he murmured. "You're too pretty."

Bram chuckled. "I'm a hot mess. I haven't brushed my teeth or washed my face since last night."

"You're too hard on yourself, too." Alan trailed his fingers over Bram's chest. Bram's nipples beaded and a tent rose in the sheets.

"You know me too well," Bram said. "We're both too hard on ourselves."

"Probably." He brushed his hand over the rise in the sheets. He stroked Bram, liking the way Bram felt in his fingers.

Bram grunted. "Don't start something you don't want to finish."

"Who says I don't want to finish?" He stroked faster, then sat up and curled over Bram to suck on one of his nipples. He rolled the tight bundle of sensitive nerves in his teeth.

Bram palmed Alan's shoulder. He dug his heels into the bedding and his nails into Alan's skin. "Yes."

"Like that?" Alan asked against his nipple, then switched to the other one. At the same time, he kept stroking.

"Please?" Bram bucked against him. "Feels so good."

If that did, then he'd do this. Alan moved the sheet out of the way. When he exposed Bram's cock, his breath quickened. *Holy fuck.* Bram didn't disappoint. He resumed stroking Bram.

"More," Bram begged. He scratched Alan's shoulder. "I need more."

Then he'd give him more. Alan moved from Bram's chest to his groin. He kissed along Bram's inner thigh then across his sac to his other thigh. He intentionally didn't touch Bram's dick. He wanted to make Bram wait a little longer and draw this out.

"Need you." Bram rocked his hips. His cock bobbed and he whimpered. "Please."

He wouldn't punish him any longer. Alan trailed his tongue along Bram's shaft before teasing the slit and head.

"Do that again." Bram palmed Alan's skull. "Wow."

He did as commanded, while toying with Bram's sac. He'd loved the multi-sensory approach Bram had used and tried it himself.

He sucked Bram between his lips and took him deep.

A groan vibrated in Bram. He guided Alan, but allowed Alan to set the pace. Alan bobbed his head, swallowing Bram to the hilt before pulling out. He fondled Bram at the same time. Did Bram like it?

Bram rocked into him. He moaned and tugged on Alan's hair. "More, please. Make me come apart."

Yes, sir. Alan moved faster. He took Bram deep before nearly pulling back. When he fondled Bram, he allowed his fingers to caress the crinkled skin of Bram's hole.

Bram tensed and whimpered. "Yes, yes, yes."

Then he'd keep going. Alan didn't push into Bram. Instead, he played with the sensitive skin. He lapped at Bram, then blew across the head of Bram's erection.

"Can't." Bram tensed. "Coming." He rammed his cock in Alan's mouth.

Instead of pulling back, Alan stayed put and swallowed everything Bram gave him. The scent of Bram's detergent swirled around him. He loved the spicy taste of Bram's cum on his tongue.

Bram let go. "Whoa." He slumped on the mattress. He panted and a fine sheen of perspiration covered his chest. His nipples remained peaked. "You wore me out."

"You enjoyed it." He stretched out beside Bram. "Or didn't you?"

"I loved it." Bram opened his eyes and grinned at Alan. "You knew how to get right to me."

"I might have picked up a few things from you." He dragged the sheet over them. "You're a good teacher."

Bram laughed. "I tried." He rolled onto his side and laced his fingers with Alan's. "I hate that he gave you shit, but I'm so glad you're here. I'm glad we took this step."

"It's only the first. We haven't faced the town. You know they'll have something to say," Alan said. "They'll want to get involved."

"If they aren't trying to already, my friends will want to."

"The support group?" He wondered about them and if they'd like him or if they'd hear about his shit show and steer Bram away. They might see him as trouble.

Christ. Trouble did seem to follow him.

"I'm shocked the support group hasn't already pinged me wanting to chat about this," Bram said. He picked up his phone. "I should've known. They've called me three times already."

"I can go." He didn't want to interrupt.

"They want to meet you."

"I haven't met your mother yet." It was all a tad sudden.

"No, but you will. She wants to barbecue today— with all of us. You included," Bram said and smiled.

When he did, Alan felt the warmth to his core. No trying to be nice or fakeness. This was genuine. "Then I'll be happy to join you."

"Want to meet my friends?" Bram asked. "Tim's sending me a chat request right now."

"Let's put on pants, or at least shorts," Alan said. He wasn't above a good naked chat, but not with so many people participating. "Who are the players?"

"Oh, good point. Dante has black hair and we tease him because he's of the devil. He's the fire starter of the group. He'll talk smack without a second thought. Tim is a dirty blond and the friendly one. He'll find something to talk about with everyone and no one walks away thinking they aren't friends. He's got a big heart and is a kind soul, but put him with Josef and Dante and look out. Josef is a former football player. He's got auburn hair, which is receding, but we don't talk about it. He's touchy about his hair, but that also means it's hard to look away. He's a good man, but he's the encourager. If you aren't sure if you want to do something and you mention that to him, he'll be the first and loudest to talk you into it."

"Nice." Everyone needed those kinds of friends. "I bet he was the one who encouraged the drinking games and dares?"

"Yes. He's great for a dare and until he quit drinking, he could chug us all under the table." Bram picked up the tablet. "Last chance to say no."

"What about Kay? And your mother? Won't they wonder what's taking so long?"

"Kay's on his tablet or gaming system. He has until noon to play his games, or until Grandma says it's time to go shopping. Since Mom's here, she might want to go shopping sooner than later for whatever she's whipping up for the barbecue. She loves to shop and he loves to tag along."

"So there won't be interruptions." He'd hoped not, but secretly wanted one in case things went south.

"Not unless the house is on fire." Bram put the tablet down. "It's okay. You don't have to be nervous. They'll like you."

"I'm used to being ostracized by the friend group." Rae's friends had never liked him. Then again, Rae didn't have any friends he hadn't fucked, either.

"I'm not him and they aren't them, but I'll protect you." Bram picked up the tablet. "Better answer before one of them tries to drive here."

"Who's closest?"

"Dante. He's over in Pennsylvania. No," Bram said and frowned. "I forgot. Tim moved to a suburb of Detroit. Either way, I don't want them to drop in. They're pistols on a chat and they can be pains in the ass in person."

With friends like that, who needed enemies? Alan left the bed and retrieved his shorts and a shirt from his bag. He'd packed for two nights with Bram, and extra clothes just in case. *Good thing.* He dressed in record time. "Ready."

"Cool." Bram fiddled with the tablet. "Hey, guys? This is Alan and he's taking my place for two minutes while I get dressed." He shoved the device into Alan's hands.

Four boxes were open on the screen. He stared at himself in one and the other three filled with other men.

"So," the dark-haired one said. "You must be Alan. You're certainly not Gil. Thank God. I'm Dante."

Part of him wished Bram would return. "It's nice to meet you."

"Good to meet you, too." Dante narrowed his eyes. "If you break him, we will break you."

"Dante." The blond man shook his head. "Excuse Dante. He's cranky because he's not getting any. I'm Tim. You're a coach?"

"Baseball, but I run a sports club and encourage every person who comes through the door to do their best and try whatever sport interests them. Everyone has some talent for sports, but it's a matter of finding what they excel at."

"Nice," Tim replied. "Sounds like you're community-oriented."

"I am." He really wanted Bram to come back. *Where is he?*

"How about football?" the third man asked. "Do you play?"

"I dabbled at quarterback and kicking," Alan replied. "I played in high school and was the kicker. I did the extra-point kicks." He wasn't the best at his position, but that wasn't a problem.

"Josef, not everyone likes football," Tim said. "Give him a break."

Josef shrugged. "As long as he likes football, I'll marry him."

"Don't think he's asking," Dante said. "Are you?"

"No." Alan tensed. "I prefer baseball. I coach Kaysen's team."

Bram returned, dressed in jogging shorts and a T-shirt emblazoned with the Panthers school logo. "Have you raked him over the coals enough?" he asked. "Don't be rough on him."

"We weren't," Josef replied. "He handled the questions just fine."

"But Dante threatened him," Tim said. "He knows Dante's score."

"Everyone should," Dante said. "Know it and accept it."

Bram snorted. "Enough."

Alan shifted in his seat. He needed to use the restroom and wanted to brush his teeth. Wouldn't the group drop dead if they knew he'd just blown Bram? "I'll be right back."

Bram frowned. "You okay?"

"Gotta hit the head." He left the safety of the bed and rushed to the bathroom. He needed the escape. The support group was fine, but he wasn't sure he fit in. They'd been friends forever and he'd just come onto the scene. They might not like him.

Might talk Bram out of being with him.

Once they got the full story on Rae, they'd certainly warn Bram off him.

He should just go. Retreat and protect Bram and his family.

A moment later, he brushed his teeth, then used the bathroom. He did need to call the club. Sarah and Clive would run the programming today and they'd be fine. They were wonderful managers and had good staff around them. He really had little to worry about, but still.

Bram shuffled into the bathroom. "Hi."

"Hi. Is the conclave over?" He rested his hands on his hips. "I hope I didn't mess things up."

"No." Bram stayed in the doorway. "You were fine."

"Until they learn the truth." Then he'd be toast.

"What?"

"They'll learn about Rae—unless you told them already—and tell you to run." Good God. He hoped they didn't know about his ex yet.

"They know, and no one wants you to go," Bram said. "You're too hard on yourself."

"I do." He closed the toilet and sat on the lid. He rested his elbows on his knees. "I'm used to being kicked. It's expected."

"It shouldn't be." Bram crossed his ankles. "You're more than you realize."

"Am I?" He found it hard to believe.

"Gil told me a hundred times that I was worthless because I didn't let him do what he wanted. For a while, I believed him. I let him bullshit me into thinking it was my fault that he didn't love me enough. It wasn't my fault any more than it was my fault he couldn't be satisfied. He knew what he was doing. He needed to be the center of attention and put everyone down. It took me a long time to realize I didn't have to put up with it. I regained my power because I didn't stop my life. That was huge."

"You're stronger than I am." It seemed like the only strength he had was on the diamond.

"Nah. You're just as strong, but the creep just showed up and caused trouble. The wound is fresh again."

"Bram." He was right, though.

"The guys approve. You didn't talk to them as long as they might have liked, but who cares? It's a lot to throw at someone. You handled it well. They'd like to meet you in person and see us in action, but that's okay. It's natural and will happen."

"If you say so."

"Who's the coach here?" Bram grinned. "You are, but I'll coach you, too. Don't give up on me, okay? I have pushy friends who can be overbearing, but they mean well. I want to be with you and that's what matters."

"Bram." Why wasn't he allowing himself to give in? He wanted to.

"If you make love to me like you did on my bed a little while ago, then I want more. Lots more. I felt alive and wanted."

"Craved." He should've kept that to himself.

"Yes. I need to feel that way. I need to be wanted and I feel that with you. I feel important. I don't want that to end. It doesn't have to."

"No, it doesn't." He had to give himself the chance to be free. To be with Bram without worries. He could do that.

"Why don't we get a shower and meet my mother and Kay for lunch? They're out shopping right now and will be back in an hour."

"So we're alone?"

"We are."

That helped. He wanted to be nude with Bram, but without the fear of being heard or interrupted. "Okay."

"Come on." Bram tugged Alan to his feet. "When I had the shower redone, I intended for it to be shared. I hate showering alone."

Alan snorted and shrugged out of his T-shirt. "You planned ahead?" He wished he had the luxury of time to do that.

"I did."

"Shared it with anyone else?" Alan hooked his fingers in his shorts, but didn't pull them down. "Or am I the first?" The not knowing scared him. What did he have to live up to?

"You're the first." He grabbed the strings on Alan's shorts, then tugged him close. "I had it done two years ago, and it's been just me in there. Kind of lonely really. A whole big shower and no one to share it with. Would you like to share it with me?"

He draped his arms around Bram's shoulders. He shouldn't be falling into the dream of having a positive relationship or even a future with him, but every time he looked into Bram's eyes, he saw something strong.

"Do you want to share it with me?" Bram repeated. He reached in and turned on the water. "I'm waiting."

"Don't have to." He kissed Bram. The more he kissed him, the more he liked it. "I'm all for sharing."

"Good." Bram shoved Alan's shorts down. His cock bobbed free and Alan gasped. Bram grinned. "You like going commando?"

"When it's a lazy Sunday and I'm not leaving the house, I do." He stepped out of the shorts. "Guess we should get into the shower."

"Step sideways." Bram nudged him first into the open stall, then disrobed and joined him. He tipped his face to the spray. "I love a good shower with a hot man."

"With me?" Alan trailed his fingers over the ripples of Bram's chest. "I like being here with you."

"Do you?" Bram nuzzled Alan's cheek. He touched Alan's hip. "I meant to ask you about this."

"My ink?" He'd forgotten all about it.

"Yeah. It's interesting. Some of the teachers are inked, but it's their kid's handwriting or hearts for their mother or some strange pop culture reference I don't understand." Bram soaped the washcloth. He scrubbed Alan's chest, then down his arms to his belly and groin.

Alan groaned. He rocked into Bram. "I got it because I love the game." He cleared his throat. He didn't want to talk about the damn tattoo. "It seemed like a good reason at the time."

"It's sexy."

"Yeah? It covers an injury." He couldn't think straight when Bram touched him.

"What'd you injure?" Bram scrubbed Alan's legs. He turned Alan around long enough to scrub his ass. "You have a great ass." He swatted Alan's butt.

He groaned again. He wanted Bram to penetrate him. He'd probably combust if Bram didn't fuck him soon. "Fuck me."

"You get right to the point." Bram nudged Alan against the wall. He slid one finger between the cheeks of Alan's ass. "I like that you don't mince words."

"Nope." He widened his stance, welcoming Bram. "When you touched me last night, I wanted so much more."

"You did?" Bram kissed along Alan's shoulder. He reached around Alan with one arm and caressed Alan's belly then situated his dick between Alan's ass cheeks. "You like me."

"I do, but you know that." He flattened his hands on the chilly wall, then pressed his forehead to the cold tiles. Anything to quell the fever in his veins. "Fuck me."

"You need me?" Bram kissed Alan's shoulder again. "Want me?"

"Yes." He wished Bram would get on with it already. He hated to wait. "Bram, please?"

"I will." Bram nibbled on Alan's neck. "I don't want to move too fast. Let it grow."

He moaned. Things were growing. That wasn't a problem. "Bram."

"I love when you say my name." Bram toyed with Alan's hole. "Christ, you're tight."

"That happens," he managed. He closed his eyes and water slid down his face. He'd almost forgotten about being in the shower. He tried to relax and bore down on Bram. "Please?"

"Soon." Bram licked along Alan's neck, then tweaked one of Alan's nipples. "Want to come apart?"

"Yes." He needed it. "Bram."

"Soon." Bram grinded on Alan, sliding his dick between the curves of Alan's ass. The slippery feel, the heat and the passion spurred Alan on. He tucked his head and opened his eyes. Bram kissed his cheek. "I want you."

"You've got me." Alan arched into Bram. "Please fuck me." He couldn't think straight. All he could do was give in to the need to be with Bram.

"Listen to me," Bram murmured. "Relax and let me in. Let me touch you." He nuzzled Alan's cheek and neck.

Alan shivered. He flexed his hole around Bram's finger. The second Bram pushed into him, he groaned. He loved the feel of being pushed, being stretched. He clawed at the wall.

"Let me in and enjoy it," Bram said. "I crave you. I need everything from you." He flexed his finger, then pumped Alan's ass. He moved in and out, prepping Alan.

Alan whimpered. He rocked into Bram, meeting him push for push. The more Bram moved, the more Alan relaxed. His entire being tingled, like he'd been zapped from within. The scent of the soap filled his nose. He gritted his teeth. The more he clawed at the tiles, the more the desire within him rose.

"I've dreamed of you, finding you, loving you," Bram murmured. He added a second finger.

His ass burned. He loved being stretched this way, though. "More." He rocked into Bram, getting himself closer to coming.

"Touch yourself," Bram said. "Get yourself off. Want to see you come apart while I fuck you."

He didn't need much coaxing. He braced himself with one hand and masturbated with the other. Water sluiced down his face and he panted. "Bram."

Bram kissed the side of Alan's neck. "Yes. Gonna make you fly." He withdrew his fingers, then nibbled on Alan's shoulder. "Ready?"

"Yes." He closed his eyes and bore down as Bram pushed into him. Once again, his ass burned as Bram breached the tight ring of muscle. He grunted and rested his head on the tiles.

"Christ, you're snug. Fits me so well," Bram said. "Like you're meant for me." He grasped Alan's hips and pushed to the hilt. He dug his fingers into Alan's skin.

"More," Alan bit out. He kept his eyes closed, but rocked into Bram. Slowly, they built into a steady rhythm. He met Bram thrust for thrust.

The sound of the water muffled the cries in his throat. He stroked in time with the thrusts and lost himself in the tenderness and passion coming from Bram. The scent of soap and Bram surrounded him. He leaned into the burn. The fire seemed to consume him from within.

Bram dragged his lips over Alan's neck and shoulder. "My God. Love being inside you. Like coming home."

He wasn't sure how Bram could be so eloquent right now. His thoughts scattered. All he saw, despite his eyes being closed, was Bram.

He forced his eyes open. His throat was raw — from panting or moaning, he wasn't sure. He glanced over his shoulder and watched Bram.

The electricity in Bram's eyes spurred him on. He stroked faster, until his moves turned jerky and uneven. He tensed. The coil of orgasm wound tight in his belly. It wouldn't be too much longer now.

Bram held tight to Alan. "Coming," he murmured. "Come with me."

He didn't have much choice. The climax washed over him. He embraced the sensations filling his body. Another strangled cry escaped his throat. "Bram."

"Yes." Bram moved faster. He dragged his teeth across Alan's shoulder, then surged one last time into him. "Coming."

Bram's cock throbbed. He shivered and clung to Alan.

Alan moaned again and came. He rocked into the wall, spilling his seed on the tiles. The orgasm had taken every ounce of his energy. His knees buckled and he appreciated Bram keeping his arm around him. He should've asked for Bram to use a condom, but he'd been so wrapped up in the moment, he hadn't thought about it.

"Holy fuck," Bram said. "You wore me out." He pumped a couple more times before gently withdrawing. He held onto Alan as they rinsed, then he turned off the water.

Alan gasped, trying to find some balance. "Did a number on me, too."

"Yeah?" Bram guided him to the half-wall at the end of the shower. "Lean on that and I'll dry you."

"I can take care of myself." Alan didn't put up much of a fight as Bram rubbed the towel over him.

"I know you can, but I'm a nurturer. I like to care for my person." Bram dried him. "My turn." He focused on himself before hanging the towel on the rack.

"Your person?" He liked that. "Isn't it too fast?" It seemed like a good speed to him, but he was orgasmically drunk.

"Maybe, but now that I've had a taste of you, I want more." Bram's eyes sparkled. "You make me happy. I get it that you have doubts and I don't mind. We'll figure it out. That's the fun of having a relationship. We have plenty of time to sort this out."

He didn't have much to counter the argument with. "True."

"Besides, there's two weeks until the official end of the school year, I've got two additional weeks after that of buttoning things up at the building, but I'll have more time for you and for Kay. We could go on a trip, or take Kay to a couple ballparks."

It all sounded so great. "We could."

"Will you keep going with me on this ride?" Bram stood nude before him. "I can't see going on it with anyone else."

"You're selling me," Alan said. "I'm nervous because it's starting well. It could all go to shit, but I want to try."

"Yeah?"

"I do." He embraced Bram. "A couple things, though."

"Yes?" Bram rested his hands on Alan's bare ass. "Ask away."

"Okay. One—you don't have any boyfriends you're not telling me about, do you? No secret lovers?" he asked.

"Nope. I live in too small of a town to be secret about much of anything," Bram said. "That and I hate lying, so I won't lie to you."

"You started this whole thing by lying."

"I did." Bram blushed. "Nothing malicious, though."

"No," Alan said. The forced error had turned out to be a blessing, really. "Second thing—Rae will cause trouble. If that bothers you, then tell me now and we'll call it quits."

"No, thank you. I've got Gil to deal with, so I understand and I'm not afraid. What else?" Bram asked.

"Last—if you ever have any doubts, then tell me. I don't want to be on the outside. If Kay changes his mind, then tell me. I don't want to let either of you down, but if you're unhappy, then I want to know."

"I'll tell you, but I don't foresee it." Bram grinned. "We like you, and we'll be honest with you—like we expect you to be with us."

"I will."

"Then we give this a try. I'm not looking for forever right now. I want to enjoy this journey and see where it leads," Bram said. "I'm pretty sure I know where it leads and part of that is downstairs because I think I heard the garage door."

"We should get dressed."

Bram kissed him. "You're the one I want. No question."

"I want you, too." He didn't see any reason to doubt. Just let things happen and have fun along the way.

Nothing to it, right?

Chapter Ten

Bram waited as Alan dressed. He admired Alan's strength. He loved his body, too. "I asked you about your tattoo, but I have more questions. You said you got it because of an injury?"

"Oh, that." Alan dressed in fresh boxer shorts and denim shorts, then pulled on a clean shirt. "I got it when I was in college and yes, it covers an injury."

"That's what you said, but you never elaborated on how you got hurt." He dressed, then stepped into his house shoes. "A slide that went bad?"

"No." Alan sighed and touched his hip. "I dated a guy who loved drag. It wasn't a big deal and it was a lot of fun going to Jack's shows. He could work those heels so well."

Bram smiled. He'd never have the courage to try drag or date anyone who did. There were too many parents that might not like the principal being with someone who was a drag queen. He didn't see why he couldn't love whomever he wanted, but he had a public job and the public liked to weigh in.

"We'd gone to one of his shows and a guy who hated drag, anyone in drag and anyone who was gay, harassed us. I tried to step in and Jack got away, but I got stabbed in the hip. The guy slashed my hip, aiming for my dick and missing, then jammed the knife in. He screwed up my playing for the fall, but I did the physical therapy and didn't manage to miss the spring season."

"I guess that's a positive," Bram said. "What about Jack? Did he nurse you back to health?" It would've been a cute, sweet ending. The very idea of it also made Bram just the tiniest bit jealous. Not that Alan had been hurt, but that he couldn't be his nurse.

"No. He dumped me while I recovered. He wanted someone who was tougher." Alan shrugged and stuffed his hands into his pockets. "I healed and hated the scars, so I got the tattoo of something I truly loved over it to hide the mess. It was the best decision because it's cool looking and baseball is the love of my life. It never let me down."

It was too soon to be the love of Alan's life, but maybe one of these days. He didn't want to be inked on Alan's body, but he got it.

"And it's a good barometer of relationships. If the guy doesn't like the ink, then he's not for me," Alan said. "So if you don't like it, then we have an issue. I won't get it removed—mostly because it would hurt like hell."

"It would, but I don't dislike it. I'm in awe because I know I couldn't do it. I don't have that much stamina." He'd never been a fan of needles.

"Then the problem isn't one and we keep going." Alan kissed him. "We should go downstairs to see Kay, and I want to meet your mom."

"Then let's go." He held Alan's hand. "I'm impressed with you."

"You are?" Alan let go and followed him out of the room. "Why?"

"You've been through so much and haven't quit. That's big," Bram said. "And yes, I hear movement downstairs." Time to introduce his boyfriend. The very thought that he, at forty-six and after such a messy divorce from Gil, had a boyfriend, pleased him. He'd begun to believe he'd end up alone.

He headed down the stairs and rounded the corner. Kaysen lay sprawled on the couch.

"You're not helping Grandma?" Bram asked. "Being lazy?"

"She threw me out of the kitchen." Kaysen sat up. "Hi, Coach."

"Hi, Kay. How'd the game go?" Alan asked. "I heard you were playing video games."

"Yeah?"

Bram held up his hand. "He's asking how your gaming went, not being a baseball coach."

"I know that," Kaysen said. He left the couch. "I got to a new level in my games. Helps me unwind."

"That's cool," Alan said. "I used to do paperwork to unwind."

"Like homework?" Kaysen narrowed his eyes. "That's not fun."

"It's not so bad when it's simple math." Alan shrugged. "I'm a dork. I like math."

Kaysen snorted. "So does Dad. I'd rather draw."

Bram noticed his mother. "Kay does love his art. He draws comic books."

"Coping mechanism?" Alan asked.

"Yes." Kaysen grinned. "I process things that way."

Bram hadn't thought about things along those lines. The comic books had always been around, but he hadn't read what Kaysen wrote, and Kaysen hadn't shown him. Maybe he should've asked. He might have learned a few things.

"I read comics when I'm stressed," Alan said. "Who's your favorite character and publisher?"

Kaysen's eyes lit up. "Well, I really got into the Hercules series. I love the minor characters and how the artists draw them," Kaysen said. "I don't have a favorite publisher. How about you?"

As Alan answered, Bram strode into the kitchen, letting them have their conversation. He hated being left out, but he wasn't versed in comics. He'd grown up immersing himself in the pages of sporting magazines. He'd loved reading about his baseball heroes.

He stopped at the island in the kitchen. "Hi."

"Hi. Did you have a good evening?" his mother asked. "I may have heard things."

Shit. "We thought we were quiet." Embarrassment washed over him. "Sorry."

"I don't think Kaysen heard anything. He sleeps like a rock." She chopped an onion. "I'm making steaks. It occurred to me after I bought the steaks that he might be a vegan."

"He's not." He sat on one of the stools. "If he doesn't like steak, he'll be kind about it and eat it."

"He's not a complainer?"

"Nope. He's a team player," he said and nibbled on a piece of red pepper. "I really like him. He's even chatting about comic books with Kaysen."

"He's hit the jackpot." She chopped another onion. "Have you read any of the comic books Kay's written?"

"Only what he's shown me. Why?"

She stopped cutting. "He's processed the split between you and Gil in some of them. His main character is tough, but he struggles."

"Oh?" He wished he'd seen more for himself. "He showed them to you?"

"He left them out and I snooped." She held up her hands. "I know, I shouldn't have, I know, but I wanted to see how he felt. He's hurt. He didn't like Gil, but he felt guilty for the split."

"Why?"

"He felt he stayed between you and Gil and messed up what Gil wanted." She lowered her voice. "He doesn't see that it was a blessing. You and Gil were never good together."

He knew that and how she felt. "I hate that I put Kay through it, but I'm glad because I got Kay and it led me to Alan."

She nodded. "Just be careful."

"Because I'm moving too fast?"

She shrugged and kept her voice low. "We saw Gil at the store. He went one way and we went the other, but he found us. He knows about you and Alan."

"And?" His stomach roiled.

"He knows Alan has an ex."

"And he ran his mouth in front of Kay?" Typical.

"No." She cleaned one of the yellow peppers. "I sent Kay to get a box of breadcrumbs. When he was out of earshot, I lit into Gil. I'm not standing for him putting

Kay in the middle. If he has an issue with you, then he deals with you. Since you're divorced, I don't see why he needs to talk to you."

"He doesn't." He appreciated that his mother went to bat for him.

"He knows that Alan's ex is dangerous and he threatened to take Kaysen away because of it."

"He can't." Gil had never had custody of Kaysen. He could cause problems, though. "Ma."

"I know." She plunked the pepper onto the counter. "He's not smart enough to take Kay, but he's watching."

"We can't stop his ex," he said. *Not yet.*

"Maybe you can," she said. "The town will not allow Gil to act like this. They know you and love Kay. They'll help you, but you do need to keep yourself clean."

"I've never done anything bad." He plucked a piece of pepper from the pile. "Kay is well loved."

"And Alan?"

"He is, too."

"Is he?" she asked. "All I'm saying is that you need to prepare for the issues and accept that there will be some."

"Then whomever can talk to me. If Gil wants to challenge my parenting, he can talk to me about it. As for Rae—that's Alan's ex—we'll get through it as a team."

"I know you will." She stopped cutting. "The thing is that this is new. You're doing what you always do, which is rushing. I never really liked Gil, but you dove right in. You're diving in with Alan. Just keep your mind on what's best for Kay."

"I am." He knew what he was doing—yes, he'd sped up way too fast. But why waste time when he was happy? Why take time figuring out if Alan was safe when he knew he was? Yes, he wanted to get to know Alan, but that was part of cultivating the spark. It was there. He had a good feeling about Alan. When he'd been with Gil, he'd felt good but always had a niggling feeling there was something wrong. He hadn't been able to figure out what it was other than he felt it.

"Okay."

"If you feel that Alan's bad or you're uneasy, then tell me. I wasn't open when it came to Gil, but I am with Alan. I like him. I'm not ready to move him in, but I want this."

She resumed cutting, but grinned. "I don't have the gross, pit-of-my-stomach feeling like I did with Gil. If that changes, I'll tell you."

"Deal." He nodded to the steaks. "Is it about time to put the meat on?"

"Yes. Why don't you take them out to the grill?" she asked. "It's on."

"Sure." He carried the plate and tongs outside to the grill. Once he opened the lid, he placed the four steaks on the hot grate. The meat sizzled and his mouth watered. Damn, he hadn't realized he was hungry until now.

The door opened and Kaysen, along with Alan, joined him.

"Hi, guys." Bram closed the lid. "Done discussing comics?"

"He wanted to go outside," Alan said as Kay strolled to the fence row.

Bram understood in an instant. Kellie, the neighbor girl, joined Kaysen at the fence.

"I see we're watching the ancient art of flirting," Alan said. "He's growing up, Dad."

"Don't remind me." Bram rubbed Alan's back. "Kellie's okay. Her mother is goofy, but she's a teacher in my building and he and Kellie became friends because they've had to be around each other for so long."

"There's that," Alan said.

"But speaking of fast, Mom warned me about going too fast."

"Not surprised." Alan leaned into him. "I didn't realize I knew her."

"From the games?"

"No, from the library. She's usually at the front desk. I didn't get a chance to talk to her just now. She was busy."

"I'm sure." His mother could be a blur at times, she moved around so much. "Was she cooking?"

"Something with potatoes." Alan stuffed his hands into his pockets. "She seemed invested and didn't need my small talk."

"That's Mom." He checked the steaks, flipping them each once. "When she comes out, I'll properly introduce you."

"Thanks." Alan shivered. "I'm so terrible. Give me a baseball team and I'm fine. Put me on a diamond and I'm at ease. Put me in most social situations and I feel so silly."

"Don't. She's new and you want to make a good impression." He hooked the tongs on the rack. "You'll be fine."

Lindy strolled out onto the deck. "Hello." She swept her hair off her forehead. "I was so busy getting the side dishes around and missed when you walked through the room. I'm Lindy Rode."

"Alan Klane." Alan stuck out his hand. "You work at the library. I've seen you when I check out books."

She nodded. "And you're a coach, plus I've seen you there, yes." She shook his hand, then hugged him. "You're doing wonders with Kay's team."

"The students have the talent. I just guide them," Alan said.

"But he's also good at minimizing," Bram said. "Which we're working on. He's a good coach and I'm glad he's working with Kay's team." And glad he'd pushed Alan to become more than friends.

"Wonderful. Let me know who you like to read and I'll let you know when the newest books come in," she said. "Are we about ready?"

"We are." Bram accepted the plate she'd brought out. "Alan, would you grab these and tuck them under foil until the steaks have rested? I'm going to nab Kaysen."

"Sure." Alan picked up the tongs. "I'm on it."

"I'll assist." Lindy nodded to Alan. "Let's get dinner on the picnic table."

Bram snorted and left the deck. He strolled across the yard to Kaysen and Kellie.

"If he's cool, then don't sweat it," Kellie said. "Uh-oh. Dad alert."

"Don't stop talking on my account," Bram said. "I'm interrupting, though, to get you to come to lunch."

"Sorry, Dad." Kaysen waved to Kellie. "I'll message you."

"Eat. It smells good and your dad is paying attention to you. Mine went to Europe and Mom's got the tennis coach here. No one's learning tennis." Kellie rolled her eyes. "I'll have my dinner delivered."

"Kel, if I knew you were alone, then I'd have invited you over," Bram said. "I'm sorry."

"Don't be." She waved her hand. "I've been meaning to order from the new Thai place. Have a good lunch." She wandered away from them and whipped out her phone.

"Sorry, Dad." Kaysen blushed. "She's a good friend."

"Of course she is. I don't mind you being friends with her. She needs people to talk to. I don't know how her parents don't pay her any attention. I worry about her. She doesn't always make the best decisions."

"I know, but I don't always either." Kaysen stopped walking. "I told her about Alan."

"Okay? And?"

"She said to give him the benefit of the doubt."

"About what?"

"He's cool and I like that he talks about comic books, but I'm leery. The last guy was a drip."

"You mean my ex-husband? The guy who was supposed to be your other adoptive father?"

"But he wasn't my father, and you might have been married to him, but he was a jerk."

"Don't hold back."

"I won't," Kaysen said. "It's just new and quick and I'm afraid to get close to him because I don't want him to turn into Gil."

"He won't." He could guarantee it. "He's known people like Gil and that's not him."

"I know. He's been my coach and I like him. I want it to work." Kaysen stared at him. "I'm afraid of Gil."

"I know you are. He's not making me happy. He's getting pushy." He hugged Kaysen. "We're in this together. Above all, it's you and me."

"Thanks, Dad." Kaysen wriggled. "Keep him around."

"I will." He watched Alan and Lindy together. Where Gil felt like a clunky piece in a precise machine, Alan fit so much better. Like he was always meant to be there.

Kaysen was happy and his mother was open to accepting Alan.

He'd chosen well.

* * * *

Bram checked the clock. Fifteen minutes until the school day finished. It'd been the most Monday of any Monday of the school year. Five students had been in his office for behavioral issues, one had to be suspended for the issue and two students had come in to make up tests. *What a great time to rush to complete missing state testing.*

At least it was done.

He checked his phone. Three texts. As long as they weren't someone else in trouble, he'd be thrilled. Two of the texts were from Alan.

Practice tonight. Schedule for postseason released. Will present at practice.

Good. He could plan his travel and work schedule to make all the games. He could also plan for if and when the season ended.

He read the second text.

I loved this weekend. Looking forward to more time with you.

His heart soared. He shouldn't be so excited, but this text was too sweet. He couldn't wait to see Alan again, too. He sent a reply.

Want to come over tomorrow after practice? Dinner?

For all he knew, Alan was booked all week, but he waited for a reply and checked the clock again. Ten minutes until the end of the day. He should be in the hall monitoring students trying to get an early release. Replies could wait.

He stuffed his phone into his pocket, then picked up the walkie-talkie. He made his way to the front corridor. Despite there being a few more minutes, there were already students in the hall.

"No leaving early." He waved the walkie-talkie, directing the students back to their respective classes.

Everyone seemed to want a leg up on leaving ahead of the rest of the student body. Whether they left five minutes early or five minutes late, they all got to their busses or rides at about the same time.

He pinched the bridge of his nose as the bell rang. The hallway filled with the tidal wave of bodies. So much noise and action. He didn't mind the craziness of the end of the day because soon, the building would be quiet and he'd be able to concentrate.

He watched the last few stragglers leave the building. *One more day down.*

"Practice tonight?" Mrs. Skye asked. "I want to go to the next game."

"Tomorrow is the last game of the regular season and the first playoff one is Friday. I hope to see you there."

"I plan on it." She waved, then walked away.

"Mr. Rode" — Denise, one of the secretaries, rushed up to him — "I need you."

"For?" He turned on his heel to speak to her. "What's wrong?"

"Gil is here."

His blood chilled. "Is he alone?"

"Yes."

Good. He texted an emergency message to Kaysen that would let him know to go to the rear door of the school, by the gym. No one else would understand the text except for Kaysen. "Front door?"

"Yes." She paled. "He wants inside."

"I'll speak to him in the office, but he can't go past the front desk. Let's go." He wanted witnesses.

He followed her into the office, past the now-locked exit doors. Students could get out, but trespassers couldn't get in. He spied Gil in the space between the two sets of glass doors.

He pressed the button, allowing Gil into the front desk area. The secretaries could call for help if he needed it and would be great witnesses. "Gil."

"You're here." Gil strode into the space. "I expected you to be busy."

"Busy being an educator."

"Cute." Gil folded his arms and widened his stance. "I hear he made the playoffs."

"He did."

"He's practicing?"

"Yes." *Get to the point.* "You're here."

"I am."

Why did Gil need to be so off-putting? "So am I."

"We're here," Gil said. "Look, I wanted to talk to you, but I see you're concerned."

"Why wouldn't I be?"

"I don't know." Gil's shoulders slumped and he sighed. "I messed up when I left you. I never should've walked away, but I thought I could find better. I didn't."

"I suppose you didn't. I'm not special, though." He leaned on the desk. "But you chose a different path and that's fine. You needed to go on that path."

"I did." Gil's defeat resonated in his eyes. "I miss what we had."

"Do you? You kept reminding me of where I needed to be better. Where I needed to change. I was never good enough." He hated being this honest in public, but he didn't trust Gil.

"I know."

"Okay?"

"You're angry."

"I'm not in the mood to deal with this. We've hashed it out a thousand times. I'm hurt. You left and I picked up the pieces. What new things are there to discuss?" He'd had enough.

"There's nothing new to discuss. I threatened to argue for custody, but I don't want to take him from you."

"Good." He doubted Gil could anyway.

"I never should've walked away, but I heard you've found someone else. I can't imagine you with anyone else, but you've moved on. I did, a few times."

A few hundred times.

"I'm doing something now that I never thought I'd do, but I'm fully walking away. I'm sorry I wrecked your life, Bram. I made a thousand mistakes and this is the one thing I'm getting right. Goodbye, Bram. Take care of Kaysen and help him be the best he can be, and love that new man as much as possible. If you love him the way you loved me, then he's a lucky man. Very lucky."

He stared at Gil. Who was this man? The Gil he knew wasn't this forgiving or willing to walk away. The Gil he knew was combative and angry. Cruel.

"See you." Gil waved, then left the school building.

Denise hopped up from her desk and rushed to the window. "He's really getting in his car. He's really leaving. He's gone."

"He's gone," Bram murmured. He never thought he'd see this day. He'd expected to be shadowed by Gil for the rest of his life. It'd take time to be sure Gil was really gone, but this chapter seemed to be over.

Denise stared at him. "He's gone."

"He is." He leaned hard on the counter, then texted Kaysen.

Where are you?

Kaysen replied.

Gym hiding with Mr. G. Why? Is he still here?

He rushed to answer.

No.

Within a few minutes, Kaysen strode into the office. "What's wrong?"

"Let's go into my personal office." He guided his son into the smaller room.

"What's wrong?" Kaysen repeated. He didn't sit down or put his bag on the floor. "Am I in trouble, or is this the jerk?"

"The jerk." He sat on the edge of his desk. "He showed up."

"Fuck," Kaysen whispered. "Sorry."

"I don't like the language, but I get it," he replied. "Yeah, he came back. He threatened something, but today, he claims he didn't. He said he's leaving and good luck."

"No way." Kaysen shook his head. "I don't buy it."

"I don't either." He still didn't trust Gil. "I'll take him at his word, but I don't believe him."

"Okay?"

"So we're playing it safe. Come to the building through the campus grounds. Go through the ballfields for now."

Kaysen nodded.

"Or go with a friend. Kellie or Liz would be good. Someone you trust," he said. "For now, I don't want you to be alone. Am I being overprotective? Probably, but I'm trying to be cautious."

Kaysen nodded again. "Kellie would go with me. She helps with Mr. K's class and I think she likes me."

"She might," he said. "When you're not at practice or with me, be smart. Keep your eyes open and be alert."

"I will, Dad."

The fear that Gil wasn't being honest bothered him. He hated being leery. "Coach Klane is someone you can talk to."

"I will." Kaysen sank onto the chair. "I knew he'd come back. I knew it."

"He says he's out and the girls saw him go, but I don't trust him. Give it a month, a couple months...a year."

"I heard he wanted to challenge you for custody," Kaysen said. "I heard Grandma. She thought I'd walked away, but I stayed where I was so I could spy on them."

"Yes, he threatened it to her, but not to me. I trust Grandma, but I'd take it more seriously if he'd said it to me."

Kaysen picked at the zipper on his bag. "So summer is going to suck."

"No." He shook his head. "I thought maybe you could help Coach at the club. Not to do extra practicing, but there might be younger players or students that would benefit from your expertise. You could earn a few bucks, too."

"And he'd be a safe place."

"Yes."

"A place that's not home."

"I guess you could look at it that way."

Kaysen stared at him. "Think he'd let me have a job?"

"I'd have to sign something giving you permission, but I don't see why not." He shouldn't have spoken out of turn again, but he did believe in Alan. A job would be a good chance for Kaysen to learn a little more responsibility. "It'd teach you to be self-sufficient and responsible."

Kaysen rolled his eyes. "Yeah, Dad."

"Okay, all adulting aside, it'd be good for you to work with sports. You said you wanted to do something in sports when you got older and this would be a good chance to find out if you really do. If you don't like it, then you'll know before you put a lot of time and schooling into it."

"True."

"I'll talk to him at practice, but it'll be okay. You're safe," he said. "I'm protecting you."

"I know, Dad." Kaysen left his seat. "We need to go. I'm going to be late for practice. We're getting the schedule for the rest of the season."

"Oh, yeah." He gathered his paperwork and stuffed it into his briefcase along with his tablet. "I'll work in the stands."

"You always do." Kaysen picked up his backpack. "Don't you ever not work?"

"No." He never felt like he was finished. "It's almost the end of the school year."

"I know. I have to study for tests." Kaysen waited for him to finish up gathering his belongings. "At least you're leaving on time. You're always here until late."

"I know." He needed to streamline his belongings. "Let's go." He grabbed his phone, keys and switched off the lights.

"Cool." Kaysen headed out to the front office.

He locked the door, then walked past the secretaries. "You know the drill. Thank you, ladies. You're gems. I appreciate you all."

The secretaries waved.

He left the building and followed Kaysen to his car.

"Why didn't you play ball professionally?" Kaysen asked. "You could've."

"I wanted to teach." He unlocked the vehicle. "If I had played in the pros, I wouldn't have been able to take care of you." He probably wouldn't have been able to adopt him.

Kaysen plopped onto the seat. "I thought it was because you were gay."

"That wasn't a popular thing back then when I started, but it'd be fine now."

"Oh." Kaysen snorted. "I bet no one cares. You're you and that's what matters."

"It is." He drove over to the sports complex. "Do you realize you'll be fourteen in a month? You'll be an eighth grader? Where did the time go?"

"Dad..." Still, Kaysen grinned.

"What do you want for your birthday?" He pulled onto the main road. "You never said."

"I told Grandma," Kaysen said. "But I want a new glove that's a little bigger and more for pitching, and a set of headphones."

"That's all?"

"A phone upgrade?" Kaysen grinned wide and poked his cheek with his index finger.

"Not yet." He wasn't ready to buy his son a smartphone. "Sorry."

"Never hurts to ask."

"Nope." Not that he'd budge. "When you start practice driving, we'll talk about it. Not so you can text and drive, but so you can have the app for the driving school classes."

"Deal."

He stopped in the sports complex parking lot. "We're here. I'm going to talk to Alan, then I'll be in the stands."

"I'm going to change." Kaysen left the car and retrieved his bag from the trunk.

He kept an eye on Kaysen, but took a moment to breathe. Bram had been through so much lately. A boyfriend, a new relationship, the end of an era with his ex-husband and his son growing up.

All under the microscope of a small town.

Hopefully, he'd survive.

Chapter Eleven

Alan finished setting up for the practice session and wiped his hands on his back pockets. He wasn't dusty, but now that he had Bram in his life, he wanted to look better and more professional.

He glanced over his shoulder, noticing the first few players arriving. He spotted Bram and Kaysen as well. Part of him wanted to be irked with Bram for ignoring his texts, but the rest of him understood Bram had bigger things to worry about.

"Hi." Bram carried his briefcase and strode across the field. "How are you?"

"Good. Sweaty, but ready. You?" He met Bram halfway. "You're busy."

"This is the hectic time of year," Bram said. Once closer, he lowered his voice. "Missed holding you."

He swore his cheeks burned. "Missed you, too."

"Sorry I didn't reply. Gil showed up."

"Shit," he whispered.

"It was tense, but might—I stress *might*—be over."

"Oh?" That could be a relief.

"I'm not betting on it, but we might be at the end of the trial with him," Bram said. "But I need to talk to you about the situation and keeping Kay safe."

"Yes." He hooked his fingers in his front pockets. "He's okay?"

"He is right now, but we're playing it extra safe. Keep an eye on him, don't leave him alone and reassure him when he gets edgy. Angsty."

"Got it." It all made sense.

"I appreciate your help. I'm not sure if this is meant to go the distance, but the fact that you're helping me is priceless. I can't thank you enough."

"He's one of my players and I care about all of them. I like Kay. He's a good kid and doesn't deserve to be hurt. I believe he's got talent, too." He'd seen it.

"Are you working tonight?"

"I am." Not that he wanted to be there. He'd rather be with Bram. "I'm at the club until ten tonight."

"Would you want to have dinner with us, then tomorrow?" Bram asked. "I'd love it if you came over."

"I'd love to." Alan touched Bram's arm and the sparks shot from his fingertips to his heart. "Maybe I return the favor."

Bram shivered and it warmed Alan's blood. Bram grinned. "You're making this difficult."

"How?"

"I want to kiss you and start the favor."

It wasn't the right place to have some romantic time, but they'd have it soon enough. "I do, too. I work tonight and I have practice every night this week, in addition to the games, but I'd love to come over tomorrow. How about Thursday, too?"

"I'd love it. You're working until ten?" Bram asked. "I have a question for you."

"Oh?" He'd love to hear this. He snorted. He was using the word love a lot lately. It was too soon for that emotion, but it was creeping in. "What?"

"I might have overpromised something."

"You have to stop doing that." He understood Bram wanted to get through the getting-to-know-you phase and into the comfortable partnership one, but they needed a little time. "What now? Are we getting married?"

"No." Bram blushed, then frowned. "I'm sorry. That sounded terrible. I mean, I don't think I dislike it, but that's not it. I told Kay he could work at your club this week."

Alan tensed. There were so many logistical issues with having Kay there as a worker, but it could be done. He'd have to think about it and have a plan in place, but there were chances to accomplish what Bram wanted. "Bram."

"I didn't say he'd have a salary position. He could do something like laundry or work with the younger kids on baseball. I don't know. I was reaching after Gil showed up and trying to give him something safe to do with stability. It'd keep him active this summer and mostly, safe."

Alan sighed. "I need to get practice rolling, but we can discuss it. Why don't you and Kay follow me to the club and we can eat while we talk? The food counter at the club makes pretty good pressed sandwiches."

"I'd like that." Bram hesitated. "I'm sorry. I'm scared he'll be taken, but I shouldn't have overpromised."

"It's fine." Alan shrugged and grinned. He'd learned not to sweat this kind of stuff. "If I were in your position, I might have done the same thing. We'll talk at the end."

"Deal. I'll be in the stands working."

"Again?" Every time he turned around, Bram was working.

"It's a never-ending cycle."

"I can see that." He winked. "We'll talk."

"We will."

Much as he wanted to watch Bram and ogle his ass as he walked away, Alan forced his attention to the players. "Okay, guys. Three laps around the field to warm up, then ten minutes of catch. Let's go."

He paid attention to the players and how they hustled or not around the field. The players honed in on wanting to be the best were trying. A few weren't bothering. They barely jogged. He strode to home plate and applauded. "Come on, guys. Keep up the enthusiasm. You're lagging."

A couple of the players picked up their pace, but Dino and Jeffrey didn't bother.

"Guys?" He tipped his head. "You're wanting to pitch and be starters, but you're not showing me why you should be."

Dino stopped and glared at him. "Dad says you're not giving me the opportunities you should be. You're excluding me and I think you are."

"Okay." He directed Dino away from the rest of the players. "So tell me how you think this is happening?" He'd love to hear this.

"You're favoring your boyfriend's kid." Dino spit to the side, sending the blob into the grass.

"Gross." He frowned. "Don't do that. You know better."

"I can do what I want because I'm learning from my dad."

"Did your dad play professional ball?" he asked. "You know I did. He's amateur, and that's fine, but he's never coached or played at the highest level. Are you sure you want that coaching, or do you want to listen to him?"

"Both." Dino rolled his eyes. "I want to play football."

"I know."

"But you are favoring Kaysen. He gets to pitch more and I don't."

"I've got you in the relief position, which is more important, if you look at it, because you're saving the game. He's getting it started, but you provide the save — if you're focused."

Dino stared at him a moment. "Oh."

"Go play ten minutes of catch and work on your catching skills. We're going to drill on-line drives and the short ball." He nodded to the field. "Go."

"Yes, Coach." Dino spit again, then trotted off.

He didn't like that particular trait, but he wasn't going to stop him in a practice session.

Fifteen minutes later, he worked through a practice game, allowing Kaysen to pitch. Instead of having his pitches over the plate, his throws were all over.

"Hold." Alan made his way to the mound. "What's going on?"

"Nothing, Coach."

"I know there is." He tipped his head to meet Kaysen's gaze. "Your shoulders are slumped and your head is down. That's not you. What's going on?"

"I'm worried."

"About your dad and that situation?"

"Yeah."

"And?" There had to be more than that.

"Dino chewed me out and said I shouldn't be starting. He's mad at me."

"He's mad at the world. Not you. Keep that in mind and focus on what you can do. That's all you can control," Alan said. "I know it's hard."

"Okay."

"I get it. I'm just the coach and it's hard to listen to me when the feelings are swarming in your head. You'll get it under control." He nodded. "I know you will. You're a good player and it's in you."

"Okay." Kaysen straightened his shoulders. "Can I take a break from pitching today and play outfield?"

"Sure."

He gave Kaysen the space to cool down and switched Dino into the pitching position. He'd have to deal with Dino's dad later, but this needed to be done.

Once practice concluded, he picked up the various equipment. Bram joined him on the field. "His pitching is off."

"I know and I tried, but he's got a lot going on in his head. I don't know what else to tell him."

Bram groaned. "It's not his fault. Life has thrown him a curveball and he's navigating it. I wish Gil hadn't chosen this time to do this, but he did."

"He did." He tossed the extra bats into the bag. "I need to clean up, but I'll be at the club in twenty minutes or so. If you go to the counter and order, tell them it's under my account and they'll take care of it." It was the least he could do.

"Thanks." Bram clapped him on the shoulder. "I'd do more, but you know."

"I do." He winked, then cleared his throat. "You need to go. Whitcomb's coming. He'll want to ream my butt."

"Of course. We'll catch you at the club." Bram sighed and walked away.

Caleb Whitcomb stormed onto the field. "What was that?"

"What was what?" He picked up the handful of baseball mitts, then put them in the bag. "What'd I miss?" He had every idea what he'd missed, but he'd allow Caleb to make his case.

"You know what I'm talking about. You let Kaysen show he's not ready and forced Dino to ice himself and he screwed up. It's not good coaching," Caleb said. "You're not taking the whole of the team into account. You're thinking of your boyfriend's kid."

"I am?"

"You are," Caleb challenged. "I can coach this team better than you."

"I put him in the outfield to cool down. How was that favoring him?" he asked. "And Dino is our clutch pitcher. As I told him, he's the one who saves the game. That's big."

"It is, but he should be the star of the team. I heard they haven't even voted for the MVP and there's one clear choice," Caleb said. "I don't see what the issue is."

"The issue is the season isn't over yet. When it is, we'll vote. Until then, we focus on the game," Alan replied. He finished picking up the equipment. "I need to get to work and the rest of the players have gone home. Why don't you talk to your son about what he really wants. He's expressed the idea he'd like to play football. Why not let him try it and see if he's better at that sport?"

"You're saying he's not the best at baseball?"

Caleb wasn't understanding his point. "I never said that."

"You don't want him on the team."

"Mr. Whitcomb, I want every player who is interested on the team. I want to use their strengths and help them overcome their perceived weaknesses to be the best player they can be. I want all my players to succeed," he said and zipped the bag. "I need to go. I'm late for work."

"I'm going to make sure you're fired. You're terrible."

"Then I implore you to take over. If you think you're better, I'd suggest you coach one of the summer league teams to get your feet wet, then offer your resume in the winter." He doubted Whitcomb would get hired, but no one could say he'd been cruel or rude to him.

"You bet I will." Caleb marched away from him, then turned on his heel and came back.

"Yes?" He should've known he wouldn't get away easily.

"You need to focus on every student. I know you're porking Rode. Everyone knows. It's all around town and people are talking. They don't like that you're focusing on one student versus everyone else. Keep your dick to yourself and do what you're doing after the season when he's not your player."

"Noted." *Irritating, but noted.*

"You're the reason this game is garbage," Caleb snapped.

"Thank you for your input."

"Yeah." Caleb strode away and this time he kept going right out to the parking lot.

Alan carried the bag to the equipment to the storage building and put the bag on the shelf. He locked the building, then headed for the parking lot himself. He wanted to get to the sports club as soon as possible. As he hurried to his loaner truck, he noticed Rae.

"You're here." *What is it with exes showing up today?* "There's a restraining order in place. Go."

"I know, but I needed to speak to you," Rae said. "I saw the practice."

"It's open to the public." He held up his hands. "Go. I'm not supposed to have contact with you."

"I know." Rae swept his gaze over Alan. "I saw him."

This wasn't going to end well. "Please go. Will you?"

"He's cute. He's more your type. You like the polished ones, with suits and shit."

He winced. "I'm not answering."

"Do you love him?"

"You need to go." He hated this uneasiness, but he understood exactly how Kaysen felt. He, like Kaysen, didn't know when the ex would show up and cause problems. "Stop making this worse. You need to get out of here."

"It bothers me." Rae leaned on the truck fender and crossed his ankles. "I thought we'd find our way back to each other."

This had to end. "Not when you kept cheating on me. I don't want to pick up whatever you're bringing home and I'm tired of getting my heart broken because you chose someone else. I had to move on."

"You did." Rae had a faraway look in his eyes. "I thought you might change your mind."

"Not today and not for a while. I need to protect myself." His heart, his health, his mindset. "I'm sorry, but I'm not sorry. Now go."

"Why?"

"You need to find who makes you happy and he's not me. You knew that all along, though. You knew your friends hated me. You didn't stand up for me. You know your family detested me and let them treat me like crap. You never wanted to show me off. It was all about you. I don't want to be the center of attention, but I want to be nurtured by my partner. All you wanted to do was nurture yourself."

Rae half-shrugged, then stood tall. "Whatever."

"I'm sorry. I need to be an equal."

"I never made you feel equal?"

"No." It was the truth, even if it hurt Rae. "Please, go. The cops will be around and they'll see us."

"Figures." Rae brushed himself off and grunted. "Fine. Then everything we did was a joke."

"I never said that."

Rae shook his head. "You didn't have to. You moving on is enough." He turned his back on Alan, then faced him again. "You know what? I never stopped loving you. That's why I came back. I might have cheated, but I never stopped. I cared about you. I wanted what we had. I loved you. I see you never loved me. No after how much I screwed up, I thought I could come back, but no. You've changed. You're harder and cranky. You're mean. Goodbye, Alan. You'll miss me when I'm gone." He shook his head, then stomped off.

He didn't know what to say. Everything with Rae was drama. Why were exes all drama? He never wanted to deal with this kind of over-the-top crap again. He was too old for it.

Still, a sickening feeling settled in his belly. Something about the situation with Rae was off. He couldn't figure out what, but there was something wrong. Rae never left this easily or with such muted drama.

Alan settled behind the wheel of his truck. He needed a second to breathe and process. He needed some calm.

No wonder he'd found Bram. As much as Bram thought he worked too much and was too boring, he brought a good sense of calm. A grown-up love to have and cultivate.

He drove the short way across town to the sports club. As he pulled into the parking lot, he looked at the facility with fresh eyes. The building housed not only a skate park, but skate rink, basketball courts which could be volleyball courts, walking tracks, a pool, baseball batting cages, workout equipment and even a playground for active play for younger children.

He parked in his usual spot and turned off the engine. A thought occurred to him. He could offer time at the facility to the school for rewards. Maybe a group could use the game room for an hour or two as a bribe for reading or good grades. He'd have to bring that up to Bram and see what his partner thought.

He snorted and laughed. His partner. Yeah, Bram was quickly becoming his partner. Good. He loved it.

He headed into the building and caught up to Bram and Kaysen at the counter. "Did you order?"

"Yes, but I paid for it." Bram held up his hand. "I insist."

"Fine." He had better things to argue about. He approached the counter. "May I have my usual? And could you bring not only my food, but theirs to my office? Thanks, Jackie."

The woman grinned. "Then here's the cups. You're welcome!"

"Get a drink and I'll wait for you." Alan offered the cup to Kaysen. "You'll want to try the fruit punch. It's all fruit."

Kaysen filled his drink as Bram filled his. Alan accepted a bottle of water, then waited for his people. "Ready?" Alan asked.

"We are." Kaysen plunked the lid on his cup. "This is good."

"I know, right?" He waited for Bram.

"Sorry. I'm the caboose." Bram joined them as they walked through the facility to the offices.

"We have a lot to offer and it's cool to see the various levels of abilities in the building all getting fit, enjoying sports and finding something that makes them happy." He opened the door to his office. "In here."

"Wow." Kaysen stopped at the trophies. "Are these all yours?"

"No, they're the older ones that the clubs here at the facility have won," Alan said and sat behind his desk. He withdrew napkins from one of the drawers. "Food should be here soon."

"Funny, I see your name on a lot of these." Bram joined him at the desk. "Are these from when you played?"

"Yeah." He hated talking about them. "They're safer here." He gestured to the seats. If they'd stop looking at his chunks of plastic, they could have a better conversation.

"Why'd you stop playing?" Kaysen asked. "You're here, not playing."

"I blew out my elbow," Alan said. "Don't recommend."

"Ouch." Bram frowned. "Teaching brought you to Lakewood?"

"Moving to Shaker did, actually, but yes." He jumped up from his seat as the door opened and Jackie brought in the boxes of food. "Thank you," he said to her. "Dinner's here," he said a bit louder.

"Yes." Kaysen grabbed his and sat on the sofa.

"I'd say thank you, but he's focused," Alan said. "Sheesh."

"Ignore him. He's hungry or as he puts it, he's inhaling and can't talk." Bram rolled his eyes. "When he's done, he'll thank you."

Alan spread the cardboard boxes on his desk. "So I was thinking about your suggestion that Kay works here. I can make it happen. We'll need you to do a permission form, since he's under sixteen and won't do more than ten hours all week, but it's something for him to do."

Kaysen stopped eating long enough to give him a thumbs-up.

"Maybe like three days a week? Couple hours?" Alan asked. "If that works, then I have another idea that has nothing to do with Kay. What about using the facility for rewards for the students at your school? Like a two-hour slot in the game room or pool? The most reading minutes or something gets the prize?"

"I love that." Bram nodded and pulled out his phone. "I'm jotting that down. Good idea. We could use money from the field trip funds or get a grant to help cover the costs for it."

"I'll donate some time for the events, too." Alan opened the paper around his sandwich. "How was work? Got everything done?"

"I will eventually, but I've figured out that it'll all get done eventually," Bram said. "Just a matter of letting it happen when it will instead of stressing on it."

"True." He pulled a handful of tokens from his desk.

Kaysen finished his food and flopped onto the couch. "Better."

"Want to play games in the game room?" Alan pushed the tokens toward Kaysen. "Here's a dozen or so games for free."

"Yes." Kaysen grabbed the coins and darted from the room. He ducked back in the doorway. "Thank you." Then disappeared again.

"He's nonstop." Alan picked at his veggie chips. "How do you keep up?"

"Not well." Bram pushed his half-eaten sandwich aside. "He's happy."

"I should've asked you before I gave those to him." He winced. "Sorry."

"That did wonders for his mood, so it's fine. I wasn't sure how to bring him out of his funk and you helped, so kudos."

"It's temporary. He's being teased by the team, and Dino, especially, because they think he's getting special treatment. Whitcomb confronted me directly." Alan ate another chip. "He's got talent and we need to cultivate it."

"The batting cages will help."

"They will." Bram toyed with his box, then closed it. "How do you balance it all?"

"This? I don't." Alan nibbled on his sandwich. "Most of the time, I'm barely keeping it together."

"I hear you."

"So, I hear. Speaking of hearing, we're getting married. Seriously, I made that comment and it's already spread. One of the mothers asked me in an email," Alan said. "Who knew?"

"I guess if I'm marrying someone, then you're a good candidate," Bram said. "I'm not ready to get married again, but I want to keep seeing you. I want to foster this. Right now, I'm trying to figure out how to get you back to my house. I want quality time alone with you."

"You do?" So did he. He finished up his food. "I like being with you, too. You're fun."

"You make it hard to keep my hands to myself."

"Then I'm not the only one?" Alan reached across the desk and grasped Bram's hand. "I'm ensnared."

"So am I." Bram beamed. "I'm happy."

"Since you brought up happy, what exactly happened with Gil, which is the opposite of happy?" He wanted to get it talked out before Kaysen returned.

Bram recounted the story of Gil's visit. "If he's truly gone, then good. We need the break and for it to be for good. If he's lying, then we know what to do."

"That's sad you know what to do to handle it, but good you do know," Alan said. He couldn't imagine being in Bram's shoes. "We'll get through it."

"We will," Bram said. "But you do know. You're doing it with Rae. Has he surfaced lately?"

"He did and he got weird, but he also left. I don't know what his deal is, and I feel strange about it, but I can't change him." He stared at Bram. "I did figure this out, though. I'm not going to be afraid any longer. If he wants to be off-the-wall, then that's up to him. I'm living my life. I'm done hiding."

"You sound like you've been talking to my mother," Bram said. He grinned. "A lot like her."

"I'm tired of being tired, but I might have had a chat with her, too." He shrugged. He'd spent an hour talking to her, trying to figure out what he wanted to do about Rae. "I got the truck to the JVS and they're going to fix it. I've got one they've done and needs body work, but it's drivable for now, so I'm using it."

"Nice." Bram grinned. "We move forward together? We're broken people, but we're finding ways to be mended as we find a common path together? I can't imagine going on this journey with anyone else."

"Likewise." His life might be in chaos, but he had Bram and Kaysen and things would be fine.

Eventually.

Chapter Twelve

Bram packed up the car after the game. His heart was still pounding. The game had been tense and exciting as the Panthers managed to win and were onto the next round of play.

He closed the trunk of his car as Kaysen trudged up to him. He held onto his bag and a popsicle. "Hi, Dad."

"Put your bag in." He opened the trunk long enough for Kaysen to deposit his bag in it, then closed the lid. "You pitched a great game. I heard a few people in the stands who commented that you've really come on in the second half of the season."

"I tried." Kaysen chomped on the popsicle. "Is Alan coming over?"

"After he cleans up, yes." He couldn't wait. He needed to see Alan. Call him a hornball, but he craved holding Alan when he slept. "Is that okay?"

"Sure is." Kaysen finished the ice pop and tossed the plastic wrapper in the recycling can a few parking spots away. "I have to study for my math test."

"Fun." He hit the button to open the car for his son. "Ready? I ordered tacos. Should be delivered about the same time we get home."

"Yes." Kaysen jumped into the car. "Did you get the make-your-own kind?"

"And all the fixin's. Should be enough for a dozen or so tacos."

"Is Grandma coming over?"

"She left as soon as the game concluded because she said she had something to do." He wasn't sure what.

"Oh..." Kaysen nodded once. "I bet she's going to see Carl."

"Who?"

"She's got a boyfriend. His name is Carl and he takes her places. He's a landscaper and fairly nice. I met him," Kaysen said. "They go to dinner and she laughs a lot."

"You've been out with them?" Good God. He needed to catch up.

"No." Kaysen crinkled his nose. "That's yuck."

"I don't know." He put little past his mother. "She might have brought him over when you were there or something."

"She tells me about him."

He checked the clock on the dash. "Well, okay. We need to get moving. Tacos are on the way."

"Woo-hoo!" Kaysen clicked his belt into place.

Bram drove home. When he turned onto their street, he noticed Alan's truck in the driveway and the delivery man was already there.

Alan accepted the box, then waved.

The driver returned to his car as Bram pulled into the driveway. He opened the garage door and parked in the garage.

"I see food." Kaysen rushed out of the car once Bram had stopped. "Coach."

Alan joined them in the garage. "Hi. I guess I'm the man of the moment."

"Sure are." Kaysen took the box from him and went into the house.

"Gee. I guess I'm not so important after all." Alan kissed Bram. "I gave the driver a tip. He said you'd paid for it."

"I did." Bram opened the trunk. "Thanks." He grabbed Alan and held onto him.

"You missed me?"

"I did." Bram couldn't get enough of Alan. "You're impossibly wonderful."

"I'm just a guy."

"Standing before a guy…"

Alan rolled his eyes. "I'm not that cornball."

"I know," Bram said. "We've got all night. Want to make the most of it?"

"Yes."

He emptied the trunk, then closed the garage door and followed Alan into the house. As he watched Alan join Kaysen at the table, he marveled at the goodness in his life. Good family, people, food and relationship. The way Alan and Kaysen interacted was exactly what he wanted from a partner. Like they were all on the same team.

"Are you full?" Bram asked Kaysen. "If you're done, put your plate in the dishwasher and get cleaned up. Get ready for bed, then, okay? You've had a monster day."

Kaysen didn't say anything. Instead, he chewed the last of his food. He carried his plate to the kitchen and said nothing as he closed the dishwasher. In seconds, he disappeared up the stairs.

"He's a bucket of energy." Bram shook his head and put his own plate in the dishwasher. "I can't keep up with him sometimes."

"It happens." Alan left his seat and cleaned up the remnants of dinner.

"You don't have to do that." He helped Alan put the other dishes in the dishwasher and put the extra food in containers. "Want to go upstairs together? Shower?"

"The last time we showered together, no one got clean." Alan bobbed his brows. He embraced Bram and kissed him. "Shouldn't we wait for him to go to bed?"

"Should. Want to grab your own shower then while I make sure he is in bed?" Bram turned on the dishwasher. "I'll join you when I'm done." Electricity shot through him as he nibbled on Alan's neck. The man was salty and sweet. He needed to be closer to Alan. Naked with him. Inside him.

"Bram." Alan groaned and leaned into him.

Bram stuffed his hands into Alan's back pockets as he kissed him. "I need you."

"Need you, too." Alan whimpered and brushed his nose along Bram's. "Let's finish down here and we'll go upstairs?"

"Yes." He let go and helped Alan clean up the rest of the way, then set the alarm and locked the doors before turning off the various lights. "Time for bed."

He really couldn't wait for Alan and time alone. As he and Alan headed upstairs, he noticed the water running and light on under the bathroom door. "He got farther than I thought he would. I expected him to pass out on his bed from a food coma."

"I expected that, too." Alan strode into the bedroom. "We have to wait a bit."

"We do." Bram nodded to the bathroom. "Go get started and I'll be in after a moment."

"Sure."

Bram stayed in the doorway and watched Alan move. He loved to drool over Alan's ass. The man had a great butt. As Alan removed his shirt and undershirt, his breath lodged in his throat. He could look at Alan for hours. "Don't go anywhere." He wasn't sure why he'd said that, but he had. "Sorry."

"I'm not." Alan unbuttoned his pants and winked. "I'll be right here."

Bram tore himself away from his partner and made his way down the hall to his son's room. Kaysen had returned to his room and was already under the covers, but using his phone.

"Hot texts you have to send?" Bram asked.

"No. Just Kellie asking how the game went and Livvie wanting to know if I'm single." Kaysen rolled his eyes, then put his phone away. "I don't mind Kellie, but Livvie just wants to have a boyfriend. Why do they keep finding me for that?"

"You're a handsome young man." He sat on Kaysen's bed. "Leave the phone on the charger and ignore them for now. You need your sleep."

"I know." Kaysen snuggled down in the bedding. "Thanks, Dad."

"For what?"

"Helping me this weekend." Kaysen closed his eyes. "'Night, Dad."

"'Night, Kay. I'll always help you." He kissed Kaysen's forehead, then left him alone in his room.

When Bram returned to his own bedroom, he closed the door and hurried into the bathroom. His breath wrenched in his throat when he spied Alan in the shower. The water sluicing down Alan's body, the heat surrounding him and the sultry look in his eyes. He wasn't trying to be sexy and did so flawlessly.

Bram stripped in seconds and climbed in behind him. He washed himself, then roved his hands all over Alan's body.

"You're ready?"

"Am now." Bram embraced him. He swayed with Alan, loving the hot water on their bodies and the closeness with his person. "I forgot how nice this can be."

"Very nice." Alan sighed. "I'm glad we have this as something that's ours."

"Me too." Bram held him and brushed his mouth on Alan's shoulder. "We've had a big day."

"We have. Kaysen pitched well and the fear of Gil seemed to go away. He was able to focus," Alan said. "I don't know what you told him, but it helped. That kind of confidence he has doesn't come solely from a pep talk, but he was able to harness it, so that's good."

"Done?" Bram asked. "I want to keep up the conversation without wasting water."

"Done."

Bram turned off the water. "You make me want to have you here all the time."

"Oh?"

"You're so hot. You could model."

Alan rolled his eyes and dried himself. "You're joking." He abandoned the towel on the rack, then strolled into the bathroom.

"Are you presenting for me?" He chased Alan until they landed in a heap on the bed. "Devil man. Got me ensnared."

"I don't try to."

"Well, you succeed," Bram said. "Need you."

"Then take me. Where's the lube?" Alan asked.

Bram stroked himself and groaned. "Nightstand."

Alan crawled out from under him, then retrieved the bottle and froze.

"What?" He stopped stroking. "What's wrong?"

"Sorry. I didn't mean to take your focus." Alan offered up the bottle. "Here we go."

"Talk to me about what bothered you." Bram sat up and brushed his hair from his face.

"I saw photos in your drawer and I don't know who is in them, but it stopped me. I realized in that instant that you've got a history like I do and it's not involving me, which is selfish, but it bothered me. Sorry."

"Don't need to apologize." In an instant, he got it. Seeing him with someone else jarred Alan. Of course it did. It'd bother him to see Alan with someone else. "You were expecting to find lube or cuffs or something and you found something else."

"Still."

"Those are photos I forgot about, but they're of the support group. I kept them there to annoy Gil, if I'm being honest. He hated them and they hated him. They've always got an opinion and weren't afraid to voice it."

"And usually, they disliked him."

"Always."

Alan stretched out beside him. "I bet they gave him grief often because he caused so much trouble. How long until they turn on me?"

"I don't foresee it," Bram said. He rolled onto his side and faced Alan. "They didn't like him because he wasn't honest. He tried to be something he wasn't and when they called him on it, he argued. You're not doing that." Not by a long shot.

"No."

"I don't think you have it in you to be that nasty, which means you're fine." He kissed Alan, not wanting to stop. "I'll show them to you later, but it's okay."

"I know."

But he wasn't seeming to relax. He had to say something to fix this. "You thought you were looking at my exes and it hurt."

"Yes."

"Honey." Bram pressed his body to Alan's and rubbed his erection on Alan's. "I'm not that cruel to keep those, but I also don't want them. Yes, I have pictures of Gil in a photo album, but that's because those images have Kaysen when he was smaller in them. He's the only other man I've dated."

"Oh." He blushed and closed his eyes.

"I'm not like you. I didn't date a lot. I was too shy to." Now he was embarrassed. He had a nonexistent dating life.

"Ouch."

"No, I mean, I'm not good at flirting or trying to put myself out there. I hate trying to date. I'm not good at being open," Bram said. "Look at me, please? I'm not trying to be mean or shit on you. I'm dogging on myself."

"You're good at talking to me," Alan murmured. "You've been so open and honest."

"You make it easy. I like talking to you. I'm comfortable with you." He held onto his lover. "So comfortable."

"Same here."

"So I open up. Hell, I've said and thought things that are out of character for me — like pushing you to have a relationship with me. I just went with my gut and it worked, but most of the time it doesn't. You went with me, which is how I knew you were good for me. You aren't fazed or upset. You roll with it and I love that."

"I try." Alan inched his shoulder up in a tiny shrug.

"And that's what's great about you. You're trying and being authentic," Bram said. "That's why I'm drawn to you. You're just being yourself."

"I'm not good at going with my gut except on the field. I think too hard and I've never been one to fit in with friend groups. I might not fit in with yours."

"I get that, but the reason they knew Gil was he'd come onto the scene when we were all living together. They had no choice," Bram said. "I forced it. Kind of like I do with you." He winced. He had to stop pushing people.

"What about when they meet me? They might hate me in person." Alan trembled. "I hate being afraid."

"They'll like you. Dante will threaten you because he wants to look tough. Tim will be nice to you no matter what and Josef will encourage you to get outside of your comfort zone. If they don't like you, then Dante will be sugary sweet. He'll tell you how cool you are and how fun. It's so fake. Tim will go silent and Josef will challenge you to a football game, then he'll beat the Christ out of you during game play. Trust me, if they hate you, you'll know."

"Doesn't comfort me much."

"I know. It's scary and new, but I've got you. I'm on your side." Bram cuddled him closer. He twined his legs with Alan's and kissed the tip of Alan's nose. "I promise. I don't let just anyone into my house or bed. I do that because of Kaysen. You make us both feel safe and wanted, which is good."

"Thanks," Alan said. "I'm doing my best."

"And you make it look effortless." Bram rolled Alan onto his back and settled between his legs. He slipped his and Alan's dicks into his palm and stroked.

Alan tensed and groaned. He rocked into Bram's fingers. "Feels good."

"Yeah?" Felt pretty amazing to him. He kept stroking. Electricity zapped through him. He whimpered and gasped. Prickles spread across his skin. When he looked into Alan's eyes, he saw something new.

He couldn't place the exciting feeling.

Alan tensed. "Want you inside me."

He'd never been the top, but with Alan, he could have some control. Not even so much control, but more like he could have a say.

This partnership was a strange feeling, but wonderful. He was Alan's equal.

Alan groaned again. "Please? I want you to fuck me. I need you."

"Yes." He let go and scooted back. "Stroke yourself and play with your balls. I want you right at the edge and want to see you happy."

"I am." Alan closed his eyes. He stroked himself and panted. A blush spread across his chest and his nipples beaded. As he breathed, the muscles in his chest flexed. The move accentuated his thin frame.

"Yes." Bram picked up the bottle of lube. He squirted the clear liquid on his fingers. "Watch me. Breathe, and listen to my voice."

Alan managed to open his eyes. He continued to pant. "Bram."

"I'm here." He toyed with Alan's asshole, playing with the puckered skin. "Feels good?"

"Yes." Alan practically trembled. "My God."

"Don't you dare come until I tell you." He wasn't good at being forceful, but it felt right in this moment. "Alan."

"Right here." Alan stroked faster. "Can't think straight."

"Me, either." He wanted to be inside Alan. He pushed into Alan, breaching the tight ring of muscle. He flattened his other hand on Alan's belly as he eased into him. He kept his gaze on Alan's and nodded. "So tight."

"Yeah, love it." Alan rocked into him while continuing to stroke. He moved in time with Bram's pumping.

"I love being with you." Bram added more lube, then eased a second finger into Alan. He twisted his digits and pumped, getting Alan ready. "I want to be one with you."

"Inside me?" Alan panted. "Do it."

"Want me?"

"More than I can say." Alan whimpered. "Gonna come."

"Not yet."

Another whimper vibrated in Alan. His brow knotted and perspiration glittered on his forehead. He tucked his knees to his chest. "Please?"

Bram withdrew his fingers, then dumped lube on his cock before rubbing it on Alan's puckered skin. He lined his dick up with Alan's ass and pushed.

He filled Alan slowly, giving him time to adjust around him. Nothing else mattered. The world melted away and all he saw was Alan.

He'd never felt this way before. Like he'd come home. Like everything else made sense.

He'd found his other half.

Alan groaned. "So close."

He built into a decent rhythm, feral in nature, pushing into Alan before pulling nearly out. The sound of Alan's whimpers and skin on skin echoed in the room. The springs creaked.

He stared into Alan's eyes and lost himself for a moment. This was where he was supposed to be and with the person he was meant to find.

Alan was his person.

Alan shuddered. "Can't... Need to come."

The electricity in his veins increased and he moaned. He was right at the edge, too. "Come with me. Let go."

Alan moaned. He curled forward and a thick ribbon of cum splashed on Bram's chest.

The sticky heat seared him to his core. Like he'd been marked, claimed.

The sight of Alan coming knocked him over the edge. He jerked into Alan. The weight of the orgasm pulled every bit of energy from him. He added a couple more thrusts before he stilled. He planted his hands on the bed and leaned over Alan. "Holy fuck."

"Ditto." Alan closed his eyes. He continued to pant. "Wore me out."

"You, too?" Bram kissed him. "This is too quick and so new, but I'm falling for you." He hadn't planned on admitting that out loud. But he'd said it and couldn't take the words back. The best he could do was accept the outcome and Alan's feelings in return.

Alan stared at him. His eyes widened and his lips parted, but he said nothing.

The fact that he didn't answer gave Bram hope. No answer was better than a flat no.

Bram eased out of Alan and slumped on the bed. He stared at the ceiling. "My brain is still mush."

"Yeah." Alan stretched out and sighed. "I don't know how you are coherent right now."

"Not sure." Bram should get a towel. Should get the bottle of lube out from under his back. Should cover them up, too.

But he didn't have the energy. "I'm whipped."

"Nah, just an old baseball player like me." Alan chuckled. "We're a pair, aren't we?"

"We are." Maybe Alan hadn't noticed what he'd said. Maybe it was lost. Not that he wanted to take the words back. He was falling for Alan. He'd found a great man and wanted to keep him in his life.

"Are you serious?" Alan asked.

"About?"

"Falling for me."

So much for forgetting. He fortified his courage and exhaled. "Yes."

"Yes, what?"

Alan wanted to make him clarify his statement. Of course. "Yes, I'm falling for you." He tamped down his fear. Not because he didn't trust his feelings, but because he worried Alan wouldn't return his blossoming love.

"You are?"

So many questions... "I am." He held his breath, waiting for what Alan would say.

Alan grinned. "Then it's a good thing."

"It is?" Now it was his turn to ask questions.

"Yes."

"Why?" His heart hammered. Did Alan feel the same? "Alan?"

"I agree."

"About?"

"I'm falling for you, too." Alan kissed him. "I'm not ready to move in, but I want everyone to know I picked you and you picked me. I fell for you from the start."

Holy fuck. He couldn't believe it. "Stay tonight."

"Where else would I go?" Alan kissed him again. "Let's clean up and go to sleep. I need to hold you."

"Yes." His thoughts exactly.

He'd found love and his life was going the right way—up.

Nothing stopping them now.

Chapter Thirteen

Alan woke the next morning with Bram beside him. He swore he heard laughter. He paused. Yes, that was laughter. A bunch of people finding something funny. He opened his eyes. He and Bram were the only people in the room.

"Bram?" He nudged his lover. "I hear laughing."

Bram snorted, then opened his eyes and stretched. "What?"

"I hear someone downstairs laughing." More like a few someones. "Do you give out the security code to lots of people? Either someone has the code or they've broken into your house."

Bram woke fully in an instant and frowned. "I know that laughter."

"You do?"

"Would you believe the support group has shown up?"

Bram had to be kidding. The friend group was there? *Jesus Christ.* He needed to brush his hair and teeth and should get dressed. He'd brought lazy Sunday clothes, not something to meet friends. "I'm not prepped for this."

"It's okay." Bram patted his hip. "Neither am I, but I think my son let them in."

"Not Gil? You're sure he's not here?"

"First, Kay wouldn't let him in and second, I changed the codes and locks. He couldn't if he tried," Bram said and shook his head. "But they can if Kay knows they're coming."

Alan hurried to the bathroom. He brushed his teeth, then his hair. He dressed in seconds, but wished he'd brought something nicer. He looked like a wreck. "I'm nervous."

"Don't be. It's fine."

"Do I look okay?" He hated this uneasiness.

"You're very handsome. I'm enticed," Bram said. "I'd take you to bed."

"I know you would," he replied. "Will I pass muster with them?"

"Yes, but relax." Bram kissed him. "Don't sweat it. I've got you."

"Okay." He had to trust Bram, despite his desire to run and hide.

Once Bram got dressed, Alan followed him downstairs. Three men and Bram's mother stood around the island in the kitchen.

"Where's Kay?" Bram asked. He went around the island and hugged each of the men, then his mother. "Hi, guys. What do we owe this pleasure?"

Lindy hugged Alan. "Hi, Coach." She smiled. "Kaysen's in the rec room with Cady and Saul. We broke into the leftover tacos. How'd you sleep?"

"Good," Alan muttered. His nerves frayed. "I thought you were out. With Carl?"

She blushed. "You weren't supposed to know about him."

"We've been filled in." Alan tried to ignore his concerns. He felt stuck under a microscope. Everyone was watching him.

"So." The dark-haired man rounded the island to Alan. "You're the famous Alan. I'm Dante." He stuck out his hand.

"I am," he replied. "You're taller than the little box led me to believe."

Dante's brows rose. "Oh?"

"But no less a smart-ass." Alan hooked his fingers in his shorts pockets.

"He's got your number," Bram said. "Figured you right out."

Dante wrinkled his nose and grumbled.

"Since he took the lead, I'll introduce the other guys. This is Tim and this is Josef," Bram said. "Guys, this is Alan. Before you ask, yes, I'm happy and no, he's not Gil. Nothing like him."

"You thought we'd ask?" Tim laughed. He shook hands with Alan. "Good to meet you. You're taller in person than I thought, too. I guess I expected you to be short."

"Nope." Alan wished he had something better to talk about. "Josef, what do you do? I heard you like football."

Josef's grin widened. "I knew I liked this guy. He asks the right stuff. I dabble in the American game."

Alan nodded. "So, which team?"

"Oh." Josef held up his hands. "I'm an office manager and do paperwork for the college. I donate time to the football program and am an assistant coach. I'm more of a college football guy, but I'll watch any game on whatever screen I can find. If it's on, then it's on. You?"

"I'm more of an in-passing fan. I like the Ohio teams and don't have a preference." Alan tried to relax, but it was impossible.

"That's fair." Josef nodded and sipped his drink. "So you're a baseball man. You played? How long?"

"I went through college and was drafted, then went pro. I played in the minors for a few years and broke through to the majors for half a year before I blew out my shoulder. That's when I decided to use my degree and teach."

"You're a teacher?" Josef's brows rose. "We now see exactly why you two hit it off. Yeah, I bet you talk numbers and grades."

"When we're talking," Bram said. "He runs a sports complex."

"You do?" Tim asked. "Like batting cages and putting greens?"

"There's a golf area and more, yes." He'd minimized the complex, but whatever. "It's a hub of activity."

"Do you rent it out, to like bachelor parties and stuff?" Tim asked. "Could someone have the putting greens, for example, for themselves?"

"Are you inquiring?" Josef asked. "You're not involved with anyone."

"Not for me." Tim elbowed Josef. "For Bram."

Uh… Alan said nothing and deferred to Bram. They were his friends and he knew if this was joking or being serious.

"Stop pushing," Bram said. "Jesus. We just got together. Find yourself a boyfriend first and plan your own bachelor party."

"You were supposed to say we're head over heels and let's all go to the courthouse to find a judge right now, so we can have a wedding and bachelor party blowout," Tim said.

"I don't like golf," Bram said. "I'd rather use the batting cages."

Good. He wasn't much of a golfer, either. Alan leaned on the counter. "Yes, though, you can rent out the golf area or batting cages on the weekends. We have groups come in to use specific areas all the time."

"There's a walking track, basketball, workout areas and even a play area as well as a softball field. You can lift weights, meet people there and have a good sweat," Bram said. "He's even got a pool."

"Swim lessons?" Dante asked.

"And swim teams. We host at least one swim league." Alan tensed. He could talk about the features of the club at length, but he still felt too much in the spotlight. He hated talking about himself, but he's also rather let the club speak for itself.

"Well." Josef sipped his drink. "Forgot to tell you Bram, we drank all your coffee pods."

"I knew you would."

Alan observed the interplay between the friends. He was the odd man out, but he refused to give into the fear. He wasn't a bad person. Just not good at being a people person.

Kaysen ran into the room. "Hey, Coach? Your phone keeps ringing."

"Huh?" He accepted the device. "I thought I'd silenced it."

"If it's your ringtone, you need to update it. It's a dad ringtone." Kaysen waited. "Is there an update about the next game? Like they forfeited and we keep going?" He grinned.

"We should want the challenge to prove our mettle, but it's possible." He swiped to unlock his phone and checked the notifications. He had seven calls and a slew of text messages. He didn't recognize the first five call numbers, but the last two were from the police department. "What the..." Who wanted him that badly? He opened his text log and none of the messages made sense.

"What's wrong?" Bram asked. "Another boyfriend texting you?"

"No." He read through the gobbledygook and frowned. "I don't understand." He switched to the call log. The five calls from the night before were the same ones sending the texts.

"What's wrong?" Bram asked again. "You're pale."

"I don't know." He met Dante's gaze. "Are you playing a prank on me?"

"No." Dante glared at him. "Why would I do that?"

"Because you do that stuff?" Tim asked. "You're a dork that way and have a strange sense of humor."

"And you can be cruel when you're trying to figure someone out," Josef added. "I didn't even put you up to it. I should've. We like to haze the new people on the scene."

Lovely. Alan held onto the phone, but darkened the screen. He couldn't figure this all out.

"Is everything okay?" Bram asked. "You really are pale."

"It's spooky." Alan sighed. He should put the phone down. It vibrated in his hand and looked at the number. This time, instead of being a number he didn't know, it was the police department again.

Bram peeked around him. "Lakewood PD? Is it about the restraining order?"

"I don't know." His hands shook as he swiped to answer. "Hello?"

"Mr. Klane? This is Detective Machado. You had a restraining order against a Raemond Pugh, yes?"

"Yes." He leaned hard on the counter. "Why do you ask?"

"Your name was mentioned in a letter on his person."

"A letter?" He sank onto the closest stool. A knot formed in the pit of his stomach. Something felt very off.

"I'm sorry we couldn't inform you in person, but Mr. Pugh was found on the banks of the Cuyahoga River," the detective said. "His body was found and there doesn't seem to be foul play involved. He left a note and I'd like to speak to you if you'd be willing to come to the department."

He hadn't been in love with Rae in years, but it felt like a knife to the gut and the air had been yanked out of his world. Rae was dead. He covered his face with his hand. "Yeah, I can make it down. Right now?"

"As soon as you can, yes."

"May I bring a friend?" He couldn't do this alone. "I'll be there. Thanks." He disconnected the call and stared into the air. His heart hurt. He'd expected Rae would do something spectacular, but not this.

"Alan?" Bram grasped his hand. "Talk to me."

He'd forgotten about the other people in the room and looked blankly at Bram. "Huh?"

"You're in shock." Bram guided him to the sofa and snapped his fingers. "Dante, a glass of water?" He turned his attention back to Alan. "Please, babe. Talk to me. I'm here."

He stared at Bram. "Rae's dead." His stomach lurched and he dipped his head between his knees. His life had changed in an instant. The threat of Rae was gone. For good.

It didn't seem possible.

One minute he was worried about Bram's friends and now this… The nausea increased. "My God."

Bram knelt beside him. "Babe." He rubbed Alan's back. "We'll figure this out."

He had no doubt. "I don't know what to say." He'd expected one day to lose Rae, but not like this.

"How about we hold down the fort here while you go there?" Dante asked and offered the glass. "We'll keep an eye on Kay for you."

Alan wasn't sure if Dante was speaking to him or Bram. Didn't matter. He didn't care. He was supposed to go to the police department. He didn't know why. He wasn't the next of kin.

"Put your shoes on and I'll take you," Bram said. "Thanks, Dante, Tim, Josef. Stay, please. Mom? Would you stick around, too? We'll be right back." He guided Alan upstairs to the bedroom.

Alan donned his socks, then shoes and barely paid attention to Bram as his lover shoved his wallet into Alan's pocket.

"I've got you." Bram held him, petting Alan's hair. "I don't know what you need, but whatever it is, you tell me and I'll do it. We're all here for you."

Somewhere in his mind, he knew the truth. He hadn't made Rae do anything, but he could only imagine what the letter said. He met Bram's gaze. "Rae's dead and I feel responsible."

"Dear God."

"I feel the guilt and pressure."

"It's not your fault." Bram continued to hold him. "His plans always involved wanting you to feel guilty. He wanted you to hurt because he was hurt."

"It's working."

"I know, but you're not guilty."

He knew that, but it seemed so remote. "Why are you so good to me?" Tears slipped down his cheeks. He hated to cry. It showed weakness and he wanted to look strong. "Everyone else treats me like shit and leaves. You will, too. You'll find something wrong with me and leave. You'll decide there are lots of things you want to change about me and you'll demand it, but when I can't do them or they're impossible, you'll leave. You'll give up on me and blame me." He didn't want to say all that, but those were his deepest fears and concerns all at one time.

"Whoa." Bram kept holding him. He rested his forehead on Alan's and didn't pull away. "I don't know what all happened to you, but whoever told you to change or did those things was wrong. All you should change is what you want to change. No one should make you feel worthless or try to change you."

He balled his hands on Bram's chest. He wanted to believe him, but it was impossible right now.

"No matter what happens in our relationship, I promise to respect you and never make you feel like you're not good enough."

He felt like one gigantic raw nerve.

"Let's go and get this over with so you can process and start the long road to healing," Bram said. "The guys do approve of you, and Mom and Kay like you, so you're one of us now."

In a tiny part of his mind and in a large corner of his heart, he smiled. The sentiment didn't make it to his lips, but he did appreciate what Bram said.

"Ready? I'm not leaving without you."

He nodded. He wasn't ready, but Bram was right. He needed to get this done. Would the support group watch him as he went downstairs?

He hoped not.

Bram directed them down the back steps and out to the garage without having them see the guys in the kitchen. In a few moments, they were on their way to the police department. Bram said nothing as they drove and instead, held Alan's hand.

When they got to the police department, Alan tensed. Would he have to identify Rae's body? He wasn't sure he could.

Bram went with him into the building. Alan forced himself to be strong. "Hi. I'm here to meet with Detective Machado."

"Yes," the officer at the desk replied. "Just a moment." He walked away, then returned a few minutes later with a detective wearing jeans and a T-shirt.

"Hello, I'm Detective Machado," the detective said. He held out his hand. "It's not the way I'd have liked to meet you, but I'm sorry for your loss."

"I wasn't with him. We split three years ago, but he kept coming around," Alan said, not able to stop himself. "Sorry."

"I know you had a restraining order out on him," Detective Machado said. "The reason I called you down was to see something."

"Not identify his body," Alan said. He planted his feet. "I can't."

Bram rubbed Alan's back. "It's okay."

"It's not. I don't like to look at dead things and I can't handle this. I hate funerals for this very reason." He was getting hysterical and hated it. *Fuck.*

Bram tugged lightly on Alan's hair and held him closer to his side. "I'm sorry."

"No, I don't need you to identify him. He had his wallet with him, and his current partner verified his identity."

Current partner? The jerk kept bothering him and yet he had someone. Typical. He felt for the current boyfriend.

"He had a letter with him and he mentioned you," the detective said. "That's what I wanted to show you."

"I'm sorry," Bram said. "I don't mean to interrupt, but what does this letter say? Something that can't be sent in a text or over a phone call?"

"You are?" Detective Machado paused. "I'm sorry, Mr. Rode. I didn't recognize you without your suit. This is a bit of a tender situation and while I understand this is rough for you both, it's better to see it in person. Come back to the office and I'll let you read the letter."

Bram stayed with Alan as they wound back to a smaller room. The silence enveloped Alan and he trembled. He did, but didn't, want to read this letter.

Nothing Rae could leave would make this better.

Alan accepted one of the chairs and sat next to Bram. As he waited with Bram, he marveled at Bram's strength. Sure, a tragedy brought people together, but he'd rather this not be the reason in their case.

The detective returned and placed a plastic sleeve in front of him. "It's not much of a letter, but I felt you should see it."

Alan held Bram's hand as he turned the page around.

I may not be a good man, but I tried. I loved them more than they know. I messed up and let the darkness run. Lew, I can't. Salvatore, I won't. Alan, I'm sorry. You deserved better. I beg your forgiveness. I'm sorry. Please forgive me.

He read the words on the page four times before he met Bram's gaze.

"He says he's sorry," Bram murmured.

"Was he?" the detective asked. "You knew him well. Was this coming?"

"He approached me yesterday, breaking the restraining order." He'd never expected Rae to do this. Sure, Rae loved attention, but this would only be because he was dead.

"I didn't see that, and I apologize for the breakdown in communication in the department. He broke the restraining order..." Detective Machado nodded. "What time did you see him last?"

"About eight last night. We'd just finished the ballgame and he approached me in the parking lot," Alan said. "I repeatedly told him to go and he refused."

"We'll check the cameras." Detective Machado closed his notebook. "You weren't the last person to see him alive."

He exhaled and the energy drained from him. "May I go home?"

"Yes, I'm sorry for your loss and you have my condolences. Thank you for coming in," the detective said.

"Sure." He left his chair. Numbness swam through him. He made his way out to Bram's car and settled on the passenger seat.

As Bram rounded the hood, a strangled cry escaped Alan's throat. He screamed. What a fool. Rae was his usual, dramatic self and such an asshole. He screamed again. He didn't care that Rae was gone. But Rae was sorry? Really? He'd been violent and cruel, yet he was sorry? He'd cheated and exposed Alan to so much danger, but he'd apologized — so it was all okay?

None of it was okay.

Bram rushed into the car. "Alan?"

He panted and brushed the tears from his face. "I don't forgive him. I can't."

Bram embraced him. "I know. He tore a hole in you and expects something that's just about impossible."

"He's sorry."

"Is he?"

He stared at Bram. "You get it. You know he felt guilty about this and expected me to be upset. He wanted me to cry over him. To feel sorry for him."

Bram nodded. "Do you?"

"No."

"You don't have to."

"I don't?" That sounded odd.

"Nope," Bram replied. "You need to get through this on your own time. If you're ready to forgive him and you want to, then do it. If not, then don't and give yourself the time to heal."

He wanted to say something, but the words didn't come.

"I'm not going anywhere. I picked you and I'm sticking with you. I know it's hard to fathom right now, but you've got me." Bram held him close, despite the console between them. "You can fall apart with me. I'll protect you."

He collapsed on Bram. He appreciated Bram's honesty and belief. He could be himself and heal with Bram. He'd found home.

"I'm sure you don't want people around, but we've got people to entertain. You can be as quiet as you want or talk. They won't push you. You can hide in my bedroom if you want."

"Thanks." He dried his face with his sleeve and regained his clam. Rae might be gone and that chapter of his life was over, but a new one had begun. He might not be a part of the friend group, but he had time to get to know them.

Life went on.

"I'm ready to go home." Alan held tight to Bram's hand. "Nothing like a ton of drama to make this super exciting."

"Drama tends to follow us." Bram kissed Alan's knuckles. "Keeps things fresh."

"It does." He respected Bram for his strength and his reserve. Other men would've been scared off by this situation. Not Bram. He took it in stride. He encouraged Alan to work through and embrace his feelings.

Bram was a gem.

He'd gotten lucky. "Do you remember how you sort of decided we were together before you told me?"

Bram laughed. "So forward of me. Good God. I'm terrible."

"You might be, but I needed that push. I told you I'd fallen for you a long time ago."

"You did."

Megan Slayer

"Because I did. I'd been drooling over you for the last year and a half. Ever since I met you, I've been infatuated. Is that bad?" Alan asked.

"Maybe." Bram winked. "But now I know I wasn't the only one pining."

"You pined over me?" He appreciated the change of topic to take his mind off his sadness.

"I did."

He laughed, needing the break in the tension. "How long were we wanting each other and too scared to make a move? We're so goofy."

"We are, but we've got each other." Bram kissed Alan's knuckles again.

"And we're not letting go?" Alan asked. "I'm not."

"I'm not, either." Bram turned onto his street. "We'll get through this and find our way. We're a team. Kaysen's with us and we'll make it."

He still felt terrible about Rae, but he knew he hadn't had a hand in it. He'd been witness to Rae's destruction, but he wasn't at fault.

Now, though, he could safely move on and find his future. He'd mourn the loss of his friend and ex-lover, but he could focus on the team, his favorite young man and Bram — his partner and lover.

He had a chance to move on in a healthy way and be free. He could fall fully in love without looking over his shoulder.

Chapter Fourteen

Bram drove the rest of the way home. He worried a bit about how the support group would handle what had happened. He still wanted to ask them what brought them to town. They'd just arrived and he wondered why.

To check out Alan?

Possible.

To ensure he was okay?

Thanks, but he was.

To be nosy?

Not beyond belief.

All of the above?

Probably.

He pulled into the driveway, then into the garage and parked. As the door went down, he turned off the engine, then turned to Alan. "If you want to go upstairs and have some quiet a while, head up the back steps and come down when you're ready. I won't push you."

"For once?" Alan half-smiled. "Thanks. I need a few minutes with my thoughts, but I'll be down."

"You bet."

Alan leaned over and kissed him, then left the car. Bram followed him into the house and waited for Alan disappeared up the steps, then walked through the mud room into the kitchen.

Bram kicked out of his shoes and left his keys on the counter.

Dante rounded the corner into the kitchen. "Hey."

"Hi." Bram exhaled. The weight of the situation pushed on his shoulders. He wanted to fix this for Alan and couldn't.

"Well? What happened?" Dante asked. "Is he okay?"

"No." He fiddled with the stack of napkins. "His ex-boyfriend who'd been a pain in the ass, like Gil, committed suicide last night. He was found on the riverbank. We didn't get much in the way of details, but we were shown a letter he left behind. The guy wanted Alan to forgive him. He said he was sorry."

"Think he was?" Dante folded his arms. "It's a huge thing."

"It is and I can't say. I do know he'd talked to Alan last night and it bothered Alan because it was odd."

"Think it was a case of trying to make amends before he did something drastic?" Dante asked.

"Maybe? I wasn't there, so I can't be certain, but it's possible." He hated to speculate, but it sounded right. "I don't know what to do. We've only been together less than a month, but we've been thrown so many curveballs."

"You still like him." Dante crooked his brow. "Don't you?"

"I do." Without a doubt. "I can't imagine not having him around. He's good for Kay and we both like him."

"Then there you go." Dante stopped him from touching the napkins. "You like him down to your guts, don't you? I mean way down deep in your guts?"

"Yes." He didn't need to think twice. "Unlike with Gil, I don't have that sickening feeling in the back of my mind. When I was with Gil, I always felt like I needed to watch myself."

"Because you did."

"I was never good enough for him. No matter how hard I tried, he'd find something I needed to change or work on."

"We noticed," Dante said. "And worried."

"I bet." He shifted his weight from his left to his right foot. "Alan said something to me upstairs before we left that stuck with me."

"What's that?"

"He said it'd be a matter of time before he was expected to change. He'd been left when he couldn't change and he'd been treated like crap for it," Bram said. "And I get it. I felt the same way with Gil. I was never enough. I'd never been able to fit his standards and he enjoyed tearing me down. Alan's not like that, but he's been through that. He's a partner. He's been damaged and thinks he's unlovable. He's not. He's quite lovable. I want to hold him and tell him it's okay."

Dante nodded and folded his arms. "There's your answer."

"Yeah?" Bram sighed. "And what do you think? He's worried you all won't like him. I'm open to your thoughts."

"We need to get to know him better, but we do like him." Dante gestured to the living room. "But ask them for yourself."

"I will." He marched into the living room, where his mother sat with Tim, and Josef, who fiddled with his own phone.

Tim looked up first. "Is he okay?"

"No, but he will be." He sat next to his mother. "Rae committed suicide."

"We know." Josef turned the phone around. "His ex is a major story."

He would be. "I don't need to read it."

Josef put the phone away. "He jumped off a bridge."

A spectacle. Rae probably planned it that way. "I'm not surprised."

"Sucks," Tim said. "He wanted to make Alan hurt."

"He did." Bram scrubbed both hands over his face. "I hate this for Alan because he's finding his footing and he was happy. He's worried he won't fit in with you all, but he's in a good spirit—or was. What do you think about Alan? Tell me, because I'm listening." He needed their unvarnished opinions.

"I told him," Dante said. "I need to get to know him better, but he's all right. He's a good guy."

Tim nodded. "I like him. He's stable and sweet. He's the kind of guy you need."

He stared at Josef. "And you?"

Josef shifted in his seat. "When you met Gil, you seemed to come out of yourself and weren't Bram. You were Bram, sort of, but guarded. When you mentioned Alan, you started acting like the guy we met that first day of college. Sweet, smart and innocent, but trying to help. He brings that out in you."

"So you all like him?" he asked. "Mom?" He wanted her answer, too.

"He's darling. I like how he is with Kay and I need more time to see him with you, but what I know of him from talking with him...I like him. He's a keeper."

His heart settled and his spirits soared. Good — they were all in agreement.

"Are you asking him to move in?" Dante asked. "I mean, that's a bit sudden."

"Not yet." Maybe not for a while. Dante was right — it was too sudden. "But I plan on keeping him around."

"You knew you would all along," Tim replied. "You knew and you needed our reinforcement. You're so bad, but it's the old Bram. You're taking charge and asking questions after. Good."

He laughed. It hurt to, but he needed the stress release. "Speaking of taking charge, I might have told Alan we were together before we'd even gotten to know each other."

Josef chuckled. "Without my pushing?"

"Without it," Bram replied. "I might have lied about being together with some of the parents and put him on the spot. They believed me and Alan went along with it. I sort of talked him into it, but he didn't argue. He rolled and it was fine."

"He rolled..." Tim massaged his temples. "Bram...you jump the cart too much."

"I know."

"Was he angry?" Tim asked.

"A little at first, but he got over it quickly. Once we got together, it was like we'd found the right place and were home," Bram said. "It all felt right."

"Then there you go." Lindy stood. She patted his shoulder as she walked past Bram. "I'm going to check on Alan."

"Sure." He waited for his mother to leave, then turned to the group. "Okay, so what gives? You're all here and you brought the kids. Why?"

Tim blushed. "Sorry."

"What?" He'd like to know.

Josef shook his head. "It was Dante's idea."

"We were all in it together," Dante said. "We needed to meet him in person and get a feel for him. We'd met Gil all those years ago and got a sickening feeling right away."

"But with Alan?" Bram asked.

"We met him and he's cool. We accept him," Dante said. "But we would've even if we weren't sure because you like him."

He relaxed and nodded. Good. He did respect their decisions, but the biggest thing was his personal choice. They trusted that he knew what he was doing.

"Is he upstairs?" Tim asked. "Did you have him rest?"

"I think he needed some silence, but Mom went up there." He trusted his mother. "She'll do what he needs. His own mother is dead and his dad was an asshole."

"Don't want my gay kid?" Josef asked. "Why do people do that?"

He let the words hang in the air. He wouldn't tell Josef how to be. His father hadn't wanted Josef to be gay, but rather to be the star, stud football player and go professional. He hadn't lived up to what his father thought he should and he'd been ostracized by the family.

"Parents." Josef stood, then left the room.

"Ouch," Dante whispered. "You set him off."

"I didn't mean to." Bram left his chair. "I can't change his past and didn't bring it up, but I can't make everything rosy for everyone, either."

"Nor should you," Tim said. "He'll be okay. He's had a rough patch. His boyfriend dumped him via email and one of the cheerleaders we went to grad school with claims he got her pregnant."

"How?" Bram asked. "He's never been with a girl, has he?"

"We think she made it up because she's covering for someone, but he's all stressed. Your situation took some of the heat off," Dante said. "But I don't know if it's true. I don't think it is."

"Wow." He'd almost forgotten they had lives outside of his drama.

Josef walked back into the living room. "Look who we found."

Alan and Lindy entered behind Josef. Alan's eyes were red, but he didn't seem as emotionally bent over. A bit of the spark had returned to his eyes.

"We were talking about thrillers and it turned out we'd all just finished the same Spano book. We were discussing the plot points," his mother said.

"And joked we needed to start our own book club," Alan added.

"We just ought to." Josef held up his glass. "Here's to escapism."

"Indeed," Bram said. Now he wished he'd read that book, too. He hated to be left out.

Alan sat beside Bram. "Hi."

"Hey." He slipped his arm around Alan. "You're okay?"

"I'm getting there." Alan bumped shoulders with him. "Still in shock, but it's progressing."

"It will and if it regresses, then I'm here. No matter what, I'm here." He kissed Alan's temple. "Well, now that we've got the excitement out of the way and we're all here, how about some actual family time? Take the kids to the pool or the sports complex?"

Alan nodded. "I'll get a thousand questions, but I'm game."

"They should let you be," Bram said. "But we'll keep it together. You've got a united front."

"Yes," Josef said. "I'm in."

"Ditto," Tim said. "I'll get the kids."

"Then let's get around," Dante said. "I'll handle dinner tonight."

Bram whipped his head around and stared at Dante. It wasn't like his friend to pay for much of anything. "Are you sure?"

"Yes. We're all brothers and stick together," Dante said. "All of us."

"Well, all right." If Dante was agreeing to dinner and footing the bill, then he'd truly accepted Alan. He met Alan's gaze and nodded. Maybe Alan didn't see it, but he'd been added to the fold.

Things were still tense and probably always would be in one way or another, but they were looking up.

* * * *

Bram collected his papers and stuffed them in his briefcase then checked the locks. One more day until the students were done for the school year. One more day to go.

He checked the graduation paperwork. His school insisted on doing a bridge ceremony, helping the students cross the bridge from the elementary school to the junior high, then once they finished the eighth grade, there was another one helping them cross to the high school. Every student got to cross the bridge, but not every student moved on. A couple always needed to take classes in summer school to advance.

He rounded the desk and collected his phone, wallet and keys. Most days, he needed to stay late. Tonight, he could leave at a decent time — and he loved it.

He waved to the secretaries and left the building. Once at the car, he refused to think about school. He'd earned this time off. He settled behind the wheel and called Alan. After three rings, Alan answered.

"Hello, lover," Alan said. "Are you done?"

"I am." He drove out of the lot. "I'm headed to the club. How's Kay doing?"

"He's here and doing fine. He blew through almost all of the swim trials and has just one left to do before I can sign him off to be in the pool to assist the lifeguards. He's learning the ropes to help there and in the gym, with the equipment cart," Alan said. "I picked him up after his exam."

"Cool." He drove onto the main road. "How'd he do? On the test?"

"Seems like he did well. He didn't act freaked," Alan said. "He's really handling the balance of work and homework. He filed my paperwork for me, by the way."

"Yeah?" Kaysen just might have a penchant for paperwork as relaxation, too. "I wish we'd been able to keep going in the playoffs."

"It doesn't help when my players were against a team comprised of older players who were obviously bigger than them, but it's okay. They all learned a lesson and the value of having to accept defeat. They're a talented team and I can't wait for the summer leagues, as well as next year," Alan said.

He couldn't agree more. "Has Whitcomb talked to you?" He'd already received a phone call from the parent, as if he were a part of the coaching staff. "Or have you talked to Deion?"

"Deion's worried because we lost he'll get his contract denied. I doubt it. We have to build, yes, but it's not like we're terrible. He should be fine. As for Caleb, I expect to hear from him soon. He'd been gunning for me from the beginning of the season."

"He could be busy because his youngest, Danielle, is bridging tomorrow from the elementary to the junior high," Bram said. "But I'd expect a call from him."

"I know it's coming," Alan said. "He's not happy, but I know we didn't have scouts at the game. Not that one or any of them. They're looking at the high school students, not the junior high."

"I didn't think we did."

"Next year, maybe, but not this year," Alan said. "They want the older ones."

"I remember." He pulled into the parking lot of the club. "I'm here and will be inside in a moment."

"See you." Alan hung up on him.

When he looked up, he noticed Alan by the building. He practically scrambled from the car to get to Alan. "You."

"You thought I'd just hung up on you to be a jerk?" Alan laughed. "Nah. I saw you arrive and came out here."

He threw his arms around Alan. "How are you feeling?"

"I'm okay. I got the notice for his funeral tomorrow and have become a bit of a freak show around here because people know I was connected to Rae. They whisper and want to ask, but don't. I keep my head up and do my job."

"Good for you," Bram said. "Are you going to go to the funeral?"

"No." Alan kept him in his embrace. "I'll go to the cemetery afterward and say what I need to. There's no need for me to make a scene."

"Brave." He held Alan's hand, locked the car, then walked with him into the club. "I'm proud of you."

Alan snorted. "For what?"

"Being yourself and coming into your own. You've shown me what the best version of you is and that makes you sexy. I'm so proud of you. Proud to know you."

"Just know?" Alan asked. "I'm not sure I simply know you."

"No?" He strode with him into the main room, then across the expanse. "What do you call it?"

"The early stages of love." Alan's eyes glittered. "Yeah. I said it, it's not tainted by recent events and I'm not taking the words back."

He stopped in his tracks. This was quick. Like so super quick, but it'd also seemed like they'd lived a couple lifetimes since they'd gotten together.

"You're shocked." Alan bowed his head and grinned. "I don't regret it, but I know."

"No. I don't think you do." He saw Kaysen across the main room behind the counter. He was smiling and laughing. He looked like he was happy and at ease.

Like the kid he was on the baseball diamond. He'd come into his own, too. Because of Alan? Having him in his life didn't hurt.

Alan was a great calming presence. He'd balanced everything.

Did he love Alan?

Sure felt like it.

"Bram?" Alan tugged him into his private office. "What's going on in your head? You're a million miles away."

He kept the door open, still able to see Kaysen. "I was just thinking."

"About?"

"What you said." Bram squeezed Alan's fingers. "I look at my son and he's happy. He's growing up and relaxed. He's becoming a young man."

"He is and you should be proud," Alan said. "You raised him right."

"I did try, but it's been a little easier because you're in our orbit."

"I sort of had little choice."

"That's very true." He chuckled and gathered Alan in his arms. "I don't regret pushing you. Was it impulsive and a bit foolish? Sure. Should I have talked to you first? Absolutely. I overstepped my boundaries and went way out of the way."

Alan shrugged. "We all do things that are impulsive."

"But again, I don't regret it."

Alan laughed and patted Bram's hip. "You're funny."

"I am? Why?" He was trying to pour his heart out.

"You're talking to me like I'm one of your students. You used the phrase, but again. It's one of your quirks and I love it. It's how I know you're comfortable," Alan said. "It's what makes you who you are and it also shows me you trust me. Remember what your mother said? She wanted you to be the you she remembered."

"She told you that?"

"Only a hundred times."

"Mom…" He worried about her sometimes.

"She's proud of you, and so am I. She knew you could be yourself again," Alan said. "We all see it."

"Even if it's too fast?"

"Uh-huh."

"And?" Bram glanced back at his son. "You love me?"

"I do." Alan's eyes sparkled. "I'm in over my head and I love it. I regret nothing."

That answered so many questions. He stared at Alan. He'd never expected to find someone like Alan and he'd lusted after him for so long. "I shouldn't have pushed you, but I did and it's fine. We needed that push. We would've danced around each other for I don't know how long—both of us were afraid to move. Now that we did, I'm so glad. I'm falling for you, too. I'm in love with you, Alan Klane, and I sure hope we can keep this going.'

"I hope so, too." Alan kissed him hard. "I can't see my life without you. Without Kay."

"Then there we go. We're together and we're in this for the long haul." He embraced Alan again. "This has been the hardest, but the easiest end of the year because I didn't have to stress about my partner. I can breathe and enjoy the chaos."

"You made getting through the process of Rae easier. I'm not done, but I'm comfortable doing it because I have a solid partner."

Bram stared into Alan's eyes. "I was told once that love was finding the right person. When all you know is the wrong people, finding that right one feels impossible. I didn't want to fall for you. Didn't want to admit you could be the one. Then I fell. Tumbled head over heels. In this world of wrongs, you felt right."

"You did, too," Alan replied.

"Maybe that's how love is supposed to work—two expected wrongs can make each other feel so right." If that wasn't how this was supposed to go, then he'd be shocked.

"And loved." Alan swayed with him.

"Equal," he murmured.

"Special."

"Perfect." His heart settled and his stress evaporated. He could do this because he had Alan in his life and by his side. He had what he deserved—a partner who loved him.

Alan slipped his hands into Bram's back pockets. "Perfect."

Yes, it sure was.

Chapter Fifteen

Alan walked out of the club to his truck. *Finally Friday*. He couldn't wait to get to Bram's. He didn't need to work tomorrow and wasn't on the schedule for the next two days, which made him happy. He needed the time off.

He stuck his key into the lock. Part of him couldn't wait to get his own truck back, but part of him did like this rebuilt one.

"You."

He tensed because he knew the voice. "Mr. Whitcomb."

"You're the reason they lost that game."

He faced Caleb and braced for the screaming. "Hello, Mr. Whitcomb. So nice to see you here. Are you enjoying the club? I saw you renewed your memberships."

"Don't try to be nice to me," Caleb shouted. "I know how you are."

"I see." He wanted to tell him to stop making a scene, but he doubted Caleb would listen. The parking lot wasn't the place to have this discussion.

"You didn't coach them. You misled them," Caleb continued. "You let them think they could win."

"I encouraged them, yes."

"And you failed them."

Not everything was measured in success or failure. "You see it that way. I see it as a learning experience."

Caleb growled. "My son had a scout there and the scout chose to watch players on the other team!"

"Ah." Interesting, since the game involved junior high players, not high school ones about to graduate and be scouted. "Who did you get?" Most scouts only came to the games for the older players.

"Doesn't matter. Scouts were there."

He rested his hands on his hips. "So what do you want done?" He might as well get this to the point.

"I want your ass fired. The teams need strong leadership and neither you or Deion can give them that," Caleb thundered. "I want you gone and I want the special treatment given to Kaysen Rode to end. The kid can't pitch, he's a lousy player."

"Stop." He'd heard enough about this. "Don't you dare trash the other players. That's not good sportsmanship and horrible modeling. You never, ever trash the other players."

"Whatever." Caleb flailed his arms. "You're a terrible coach. You don't foster a sense of winning. They should be cutthroat about winning. Only the winner gets to succeed."

He fortified himself. "Are you done?" His line of reasoning was silly.

"What?" Caleb screamed. "Don't you get it?"

"I do."

"Then resign."

"No."

"No? I'm calling for your resignation. I will not allow my son to play under you."

"Then don't."

Caleb glared at him. "I can do a better job of coaching than you are."

"I see." This was getting old. He kept his voice calm and even.

"You're not worthy of coaching my student," Caleb screamed.

"Fine."

"You'll cut him because you're angry with me and that's not fair."

"I never said that." And didn't do that sort of thing.

"You're going to do it."

"Enough." He couldn't listen to this any longer. "You believe you can do my job better than I can, then fine. Pick up a summer league team. Coach them. Will you succeed in every game? Maybe, but maybe not. You might, as we did, come up against a team that's bigger and faster. What will you do if you don't win? Punish them? Or learn from it?"

"Yes."

He crooked his brow. "Which? If you plan on punishing them, then expect a slump. The fear of not winning and failing will become rampant."

"No, it won't. They'll want to win for me."

"Because you're you?"

"Because I yell the loudest."

"I see." He wasn't getting through to Caleb. "Do they respect you?"

"What?"

"Do they respect you? If you're punishing and yelling?"

"They will. I'll demand it."

"Through screaming? Yelling? Dominating?"

"Rewards for good players and laps for the ones who suck."

Those who suck... "Well, expect the whole team to do laps and the ones you feel are best will only do well because they've been given prizes. It will foster favoritism and animosity among the players, as well as foster resentment."

"You're full of shit."

Right. He hadn't made a dent. "When were you on a professional team?"

"You were only there for two years."

"When did you make the pros?"

"Shut up."

Caleb was making his point for him. "If you went pro, then we'll continue this argument. Until then, I'm sorry you're upset, but I'm not resigning. I have a lot of building to do with this team and look forward to keeping the good players as well as the spirit of excitement going."

"To resign?"

"Caleb, try the summer league. Come back in the fall and let me know how it went. You might be surprised," Alan said. "Now, I truly have to go. I have an appointment."

"With?"

"It's not your business."

"Who?" Caleb demanded.

"I'm meeting with someone," Alan said. "Caleb, you're trying to control this whole situation so it's the most beneficial for your son. I get that. You want him to be successful. I want every player to be successful as well. Sometimes we have to fail to learn. You only grow when you overcome a failure. He failed a bit and figured it out. So did the rest of the team. They will learn from this and come back even better. Next season will be great."

Caleb glared at him and shook his head. "You're full of shit. I'll go and find a summer team and we'll beat you in every matchup. I'll win and you'll be dumped. Mark my words."

"Sure. Thank you." He opened his truck door. "Enjoy your evening."

"You're dismissing me? This is how you fail them. You dismiss people."

"Then show me how you'd do it better with your team. Good evening." He settled on the seat, then closed the door. He refused to argue any further with this bully. He waited for Caleb to walk away before he left the lot.

He hadn't heard the last of this from Caleb, but hopefully Caleb would come to realize his bravado wasn't working. Once Caleb found out how difficult it'd be to coach, he might understand better. He might not ever get it, but he'd have to get there on his own.

Alan rolled his window down and enjoyed the breeze on his face, plus the music playing. He'd learned the hard way how to coach and how not to get players to excel. It wasn't easy. Until Caleb failed, he'd never learn.

Right now, Caleb didn't matter. Getting to Bram and enjoying his weekend did.

He drove to Bram's and grinned. Now that the school year was over, Kaysen had summer league baseball coming and he'd been asked to help with the team, but Alan would be able to spend time with both Kaysen and Bram. He'd get the chance to find out what made Bram tick. Deion wasn't losing his job, either. Not that Caleb knew, but they'd both been given three-year extensions on their contracts. They could build the team and keep the momentum going.

He parked in the turnaround and left the truck. Back at the condo, he hadn't known his neighbors, but here, he felt like he'd become part of the block. He waved to Mr. Bream.

"How's next year's team going to be?" Mr. Bream asked. He leaned on his broom. "I mowed today and need to blow the driveway off."

"That's okay. You'll get it done," Alan said. "I hope next year goes well. I have lofty goals for the players, but we've got great prospects in the pipeline and I'll work with the summer leagues so I can see the talent progress."

"Very smart. I knew you'd have a plan." Mr. Bream nodded and flexed his hands on the broom. "I've got tomatoes coming on in the next month and I'll make sure you and Bram get some. I heard Bram likes them."

"He has a salad every day for lunch."

"Better than the garbage served in the cafeteria. My grandson tells me about what they serve and it sounds terrible."

He hadn't eaten in the cafeteria, but doubted the food was that terrible. "Are you going to watch a movie tonight with your wife? I heard she's looking forward to the newest Leo Pickens movie."

"Oh, she's got a thing for him." Mr. Bream laughed. "We will, though. Are you and Bram having a date? The school year is over, isn't it?"

Coaching Love

"As of today, it is. I'm not sure what we're doing tonight." The last he knew, Kaysen was at his grandmother's house for the evening.

"I hope you have a whopper of a night," Mr. Bream said. "It's good to see the spring back in Bram's step."

"Nice to hear that." Alan twiddled with his keys. "Have a good night and enjoy the movie."

"We will. You have a good night, too." Mr. Bream waved.

Alan headed into the house. He let himself in through the man door connected to the garage, then locked the door behind him and going into the mud room.

He swore he heard music playing. "Bram?"

"In here."

He abandoned his shoes and keys in the mud room, then left his phone and wallet on the counter in the kitchen. Where was Bram? He wandered through the house to the living room. No Bram. He went into the hallway leading to the rec room.

Bram stood in the middle of the space. He held flowers and had twinkle lights, which glowed in the room. "Hello, lover."

"Hello." He rushed into Bram's embrace. He held him close and breathed Bram in. "I'm so glad to see you."

"Missed me?"

He swayed with Bram, moving to the music. "I did. Felt like the day dragged." He practically counted the minutes until he could get to Bram.

Bram offered him the flowers. "For you."

"So romantic. Thank you." He'd never been given flowers before. "These are beautiful." He breathed in the scent of the daisies and roses.

234

"Thank you. One of the parents owns a flower shop and I decided to stop on my way home. I was going to buy you some chocolates, but I wasn't sure which you'd like."

"Any?" He kissed Bram. "I'm easy."

"No, you're not. You're a man of worth and character." Bram rested his forehead on Alan's. He toyed with the short hairs at the back of Alan's head.

The tickle lulled Alan. He closed his eyes and enjoyed being touched. His blood heated and he groaned. His nerve endings sizzled. He wanted this moment to last forever.

"Alan?"

"Yeah?" He opened his eyes and met Bram's gaze. "I love this surprise. The lights, flowers and music are all so romantic." He felt a little lightheaded with excitement.

"I wanted you to feel important."

"I do."

"You're loved." Bram brushed his nose along Alan's. "And wanted."

"I want you, too." He slipped his free hand into Bram's back pocket. "What do you have planned for tonight?"

"Some of this." Bram traced the line of Alan's jaw while they swayed. He curled his fingers under Alan's chin. "A little of this." He kissed him, swiping his tongue across Alan's lips.

Alan opened to him. Blood rushed to his dick. The first rush of desire hit him hard. He grinded on Bram. Christ, he was ready to go. He needed to be naked with Bram—right now.

"Want me?" Bram asked.

"Yes." He sighed. He rubbed the growing bulge in his jeans against the one in Bram's trousers. He panted. "Want to be naked with you."

"Then let's get naked." Bram took the flowers from him and left them on the coffee table. He set the alarm in the house, then grabbed Alan's hand. "Wait until you see upstairs."

"Oh?" He couldn't wait. Romance like this hadn't happened to him before.

Alan rushed to keep up with him. He tripped up the stairs and laughed at himself. "I'm so clumsy."

"So?" Bram opened the bedroom door.

More twinkle lights shimmered. He'd left rose petals on the bed and the scent of cologne hung in the air. "Bram."

"Yes?" Bram embraced him from behind. He rested his chin on Alan's shoulder. "Like it?"

"Love it." He caressed Bram's hands.

"I wanted to give you the romantic date you might not have ever gotten before. It's cliche, with the roses and lights, but it seemed good at the moment."

"It's perfect." He turned in Bram's arms. "Thank you. I love you."

"I love you, too." Bram yanked on Alan's shirt tail. "Right now, I want you naked."

"Yes." He wrestled free from Bram and tugged his shirt over his head. Within minutes, he'd unbuttoned his pants and shoved both them and his underwear down his legs. He kicked out of the wadded-up clothing, then crawled onto the bed.

The world righted around him. This was where he was supposed to be. Bram joined him, crawling on top of him. He kissed Alan and blew his mind. Everything seemed to sizzle. Like he was electrified from within.

He sucked on Bram's tongue, not able to get enough of Bram.

"Yes," Bram said between kisses. He touched Alan's chest, then tweaked one of his nipples and tugged on the sensitive peak.

Alan trembled. "Oh fuck." He gasped for air. "Want to taste you." He nudged Bram's hip. "Turn around."

"Yes." Bram slid off him long enough to switch positions and wriggled his hips over Alan's face. His cock bobbed against Alan's lips.

"That's what I want." Alan sucked on Bram's dick, moving his head and delighting in the musky scent. He toyed with Bram's balls, trying to heighten his sensations.

At the same time, Bram licked and nibbled on Alan's dick.

Being blown while he blew Bram was almost more than Alan could handle. He shivered and dug his nails into Bram's hip. He wanted more. To come apart. The springs creaked and the soft light added to the ambiance of the moment.

Alan couldn't think straight. He wanted the moment to last, but the beginning of the orgasm was already starting. His muscles twitched and he groaned around Bram's cock.

Bram pulled back. "I want to be inside you."

He wanted to answer, but the words were gone. He simply tried to catch his breath as Bram moved. There was no point in bothering to look at what Bram was doing. He knew.

Alan rolled onto his stomach and propped himself on his hands and knees. He reached between his legs and stroked himself while he waited for Bram. In a few moments, he'd find bliss and be one with the man he loved.

"Don't you come apart without me." Bram swatted Alan's ass, then settled behind him.

Alan couldn't see anything Bram was doing and didn't care. He knew what was about to happen. As the cool lube slid down the crack of his ass, he groaned and tried his damnedest to relax. A cry built in his throat. The more he stroked himself, the more he wanted to come.

Bram pushed the lube into Alan's hole. "You're so tight and I love it. It's like the first time every time."

"Love you being inside me." He pushed back against Bram's finger in his ass. "Don't make me wait."

"So needy." Bram chuckled and continued to pump into Alan. "Are you ready for me? Want me?"

"Always." He closed his eyes and embraced the good feelings swarming his body. He dug his toes into the bedding. "Fuck me."

"Yes, my love." Bram eased out of him, then squirted more chilly lube over Alan's hole. "Breathe for me. Relax and let me in."

"Yes." He let the word draw out as Bram pushed his dick into Alan's ass. The fullness stretched and burned, but the pain morphed into pleasure in seconds. He'd never experienced anything like this, except with Bram. In a few moments, Bram built into a steady rhythm. The sound of skin on skin echoed in the room. Alan dug his fingers into Alan's hips. He took control over the action, ratcheting up his pace.

Alan met him thrust for thrust, matching his strokes with them. His brain buzzed with the onslaught of orgasmic tingles. He groaned. "Fuck. Bram." He loved being one with the man of his heart. One body, one mind, one soul moving together. Perfection.

"Here." Bram slammed into him, pushing him into the mattress. "Christ, I'm right on the edge. This is going too fast."

"Don't care." He managed to toy with his balls with his free hand. The combination of sensations — his hands giving him pleasure and Bram fucking him — it was too much for him. Alan tumbled right over the edge. He cried out as he came. His entire body vibrated. Everything seemed to move in slow motion.

The world blurred and nothing mattered but being with Bram.

"Fuck me." Bram surged into Alan once more, then clawed at Alan's hips. His cock throbbed as he came. "Jesus Christ."

He basked in the afterglow of orgasm with Bram deep in his ass. Bram slumped onto his back, lying on top of Alan.

"Was it that good?" Alan asked. He opened his eyes. His knees buckled and he settled on the bed, smearing his cum onto his own belly. For once, he didn't mind the sticky mess.

"Yes." Bram kissed Alan's shoulder, then pulled out slowly before rolling off Alan and onto the bed. He panted and palmed Alan's backside. "Sorry if I dug in too hard."

"I don't mind." Being marked by Bram was the least of his worries. He slid his arm across Bram's belly. "I spent the time with you and that was the best part."

"Yeah?" Bram met his gaze. "I love you."

"I found my missing piece when I met you. I wish I'd have known then that things would be this good. I would've made a move sooner."

"Nah, you had to wait for the right pitch." He toyed with the ripples of Bram's abs. "When the right one came, you swung and knocked it out of the park?"

"I did. I got the home run of my dreams." Bram grinned. "I know it's fast, but I can't see myself with anyone else. I don't want you to move in until you're ready, but I have keys for you. I have the code for you. Kaysen can't wait for tomorrow so we can all hang out."

"I'd love that, too." Things were falling into place.

"We take our time and continue to fall in love, but this is you and me. We figure this out. We're going the distance," Bram said. "No one else."

"No one else." He laced his fingers with Bram's and held tight. "My partner."

"The best teammate I could ever have." Bram sighed. "Rest, then round two?"

"You read my mind." Alan laughed with Bram, happy he'd found not only his heart and partner, but the man he'd been destined to have. No more lonely nights or ragged days. Just the chance at forever and the time to make it work right.

The home run they both deserved to win the game of romance. The game of desire. He might be the coach, but Bram's determination to coach him into falling in love worked and now that had forever to enjoy it.

Want to see more from this author?
Here's a taster for you to enjoy!

Daddy Needs a Date:
Tackling Love
Megan Slayer

Excerpt

A whole world of people and no one interested in me. Josef Davis stared out at the football field, lost in his thoughts. He shouldn't be worried about finding a lover. Hell, he barely liked dating. The act of going out wasn't so bad, but it was the small talk. The trying to figure out if someone liked him in return. That was the tiring part. That and the idea that the people he'd come to know didn't try to be honest.

Well, except for the team...and the support group. His friends had been the best people in his life because they'd been honest and hadn't minced words in an effort to be nice. They were simply as advertised. So was the football team and coaching staff. He had his support group of best friends who were like his brothers and found a family among the coaches.

"You look deep in your head," Sylus said. He elbowed Josef. "We've got a practice to coach. You need to be present."

"I am." *Not wholly, but whatever.* "I'm here."

"Are you?" Sylus tipped his head. He removed his hat, then scratched his head before putting the cap back on. His blue eyes narrowed. "You haven't been yourself lately. Even the boys have asked. They want to

Sign up for our newsletter and find out about all our romance book releases, eBook sales and promotions, sneak peeks and FREE romance books!

know when Uncle Josef will come over to play. What gives?"

He had to be honest with himself and Sylus. He'd known Sylus since he'd come to the team over ten years ago and had been there since his head coach's sons were born. He nodded. "I'm trying to sort out my personal life."

"What personal life? You don't have one. You don't go out. Don't talk about yourself outside of the game. Don't bring anyone along to the parties. It's like you're afraid to admit you want someone."

"Maybe I am." He hadn't meant to say that, but the smart remark tumbled right out. "Sorry." This wasn't the time to discuss his personal life. He should be focusing on the game.

"Don't have to be sorry. The assistants are running this part of the practice. I'm worried about you. You're running yourself ragged trying to run away from everything. The more you insulate yourself, the less you're going to be happy." Sylus folded his arms. "Have you talked to the support group?"

He'd forgotten Sylus knew about his college friends. "No." He should have a chat with them. A nice, long video chat where they could talk about...stuff. Tim, Dante and Bram knew him better than anyone. They could see through his bullshit in seconds, then turn around and offer the kind of support only someone who'd been there through the rough times can give.

"Then you'd better call them. Why don't you head out? It's Templeton's turn to clean up after practice," Sylus said. "He owes me anyway. He keeps getting out of ensuring the practice gear is clean. You'd think he doesn't want to know how to run a washing machine."

"He doesn't." He knew Templeton. The guy put laziness to new levels. "Is that a demand?"

"Yes." Sylus nudged Josef's shoulder. "I have the feeling you've got more on your mind than your dating situation and it's that stuff you won't discuss, so talk to them. I need your head in the game for this weekend's matchup versus Academy. We've got their number, but you're our best play caller. Think you can get yourself sorted out enough for this weekend?"

"I can." He laughed to hide his discomfort.

"Then go." Sylus shooed him away. "Go. You need to be ready. I need my coach."

"Noted." He clapped Sylus on the shoulder, then walked away. He hated that Sylus knew him so well, but he appreciated that his coach was directing him to take positive steps in his life.

He'd become good at burying his feelings. If no one knew he was upset, then they'd leave him alone. If they didn't know he had things wrong, then they'd give him space. But he'd hidden so much that he'd pushed people away. No one wanted to try to get close.

Not that he'd let them.

Except the support group.

He headed out to his car. He didn't live anywhere close to the guys, but with a few taps, he'd have them in his living room. He drove from the practice facility to the freeway and along the beltway around town to his housing development.

When he'd thought he'd be in professional football for the rest of his life, he'd bragged he wasn't about to live in a house. He'd have a bus. Wasn't going to have roots.

Look at him now. He had a house in the 'burbs, a car and truck, enough electronics to keep himself busy and three bedrooms for one man. *How sad.*

It was time to talk to the support group.

He drove from the beltway to the main road leading to his development, then down his side street. Within ten minutes, he pulled into his driveway before parking in the garage. He shook his head as he killed the engine and the clunky garage door shut. There was no personality in his house. All white exterior, bland grey sidewalk. No flowers — he hadn't been blessed with a green thumb, no colorful statuary, no flags — he hadn't had time to put them up and couldn't decide which he wanted to showcase.

Inside wasn't much better. It certainly looked like a bachelor lived there. He had just enough furniture for his own use and nothing more. He didn't have photos on the wall, even though he had plenty of snapshots on his computer. The desire to print the images hadn't crossed his mind. He didn't even have a room displaying his various jerseys, awards and team paraphernalia from his playing and coaching careers.

Why be reminded of past glory?

He left the car and headed into the house. He'd take the truck to practice tomorrow. The vehicle required too much fuel, but he liked the way it rumbled down the road.

He left his keys in the bowl, then kicked out of his shoes before strolling through the kitchen where he picked up an apple. He made his way to his office. Of all the rooms in his home, this one had the most personality.

He'd left his tablet on the charger and removed the cord before leaving the office. No one needed to see the piles of papers or clutter. The support group wouldn't say anything about it, but he didn't like having the mess in the background.

Josef removed his socks on the way to the living room and left the socks on the floor by his armchair. He'd get the rumpled articles of clothing later.

As he settled on the worn leather, he tapped to light up the screen. Within a few moments, he'd set up the chat windows. He hadn't bothered to give the others a chance to accept or decline. He simply demanded they show up.

The first screen to open was Dante's. He laughed. "It took you long enough."

"Took me?" he asked. "How so? I called the chat."

"I know, and I've been waiting on this." Dante shook his head. "Finally ready to open up?"

He wanted to feign not knowing what Dante meant, but why bother? Dante was smarter than he looked and had a biting sense of humor. If he knew Josef was struggling, he'd give him hell until he admitted it to himself. "Maybe."

"What happened?" Dante asked. "You don't crack this easily. Did you meet someone?" his eyes widened.

He didn't want to give Dante this power, but he hadn't met anyone. "Stop. You're thinking too hard. I'm just...I wanted to talk to you all." God, he had to stop avoiding the situation.

"You're so full of shit," Dante replied. "If you haven't met someone, then you want to."

Tim saved him from having to answer. Just as well. He didn't want to have to tell each of his friends individually.

Tim waved. "Stranger! Where've you been?"

"Coaching." This he could answer. "We're five and one this year and a good bet to make the playoffs. We've had our toughest game against the Cougars, so this should be easy. The remainder of the schedule isn't as bad, even for teams within our division. We've got a stout quarterback and he's healthy this year. The line's strong and I can't complain." He'd said a lot and hadn't really answered the question.

"So you've been neck-deep in the game. What about your personal life?" Dante asked. "Gone out recently?"

"Not everyone has to club like you." Josef scrubbed the back of his neck and rested the tablet on his lap. "I like being quiet."

"Except when you're on the sidelines," Tim said. "I've seen you. You're so animated."

"I get into the game." What was wrong with that?

"Get into it?" Tim asked. "You've been this involved since college. I've got video somewhere of you on the sidelines when you went pro practically hopping around to get the attention of the team. It could be said your sportsmanship at the time was original."

"So?" He had been too enthusiastic and angry on the sidelines in his playing days. He had an idea how the game should be going and hated when no one listened to him...which was why he'd gotten into coaching.

"So you don't have any prospects for a boyfriend?" Dante asked. "Or you're not trying?"

"Are you?" he challenged. "You're still single."

"Only our Bram has connected," Tim said. He sighed and shrugged. "I'm not finding anyone either. It's like I can't seem to attract anyone who wants to be with a single dad."

Josef bristled. He hadn't tried to have kids because he hadn't believed he'd make a good parent. "At least you're trying."

Bram entered the chat. He appeared to still be at school and in his dimly lit office. He adjusted the light. "Sorry. I had meetings after school. Seems like it's never-ending. What'd I miss?"

"Josef wants a date," Dante said. "And he's ready to talk about his issues."

Jesus Christ. He hadn't said any of those things. He wasn't ready to discuss anything. Okay, maybe he was, but not with Dante's pushing. He could count on his friend to force them all to confront what needed to be discussed, but his bulldozer methods often left a little to be desired.

"Uh…" Bram frowned. "Josef?"

Tim leaned in closer to the screen. "We know you've been struggling. Have you been talking to your therapist?"

He was so used to them supporting each other and him not being the one in need. But now it was his turn and their overwhelming backing surprised and relieved him. They knew him so well. "Guys."

"That's why you're seeing Mark. He's helping and he's right," Dante said. "You're being bogged down by the past and you can't change it, so make the future what you want."

Why did Dante have to remember that?

"It's okay to discuss it with us. We know some of what happened, witnessed other parts of it and aren't going to judge you," Bram said. "It's hard to let go."

He had to give that to Bram. Of all the men in the group, Bram knew the heartache of being screwed over and had even managed to come out on the other side. Every time he saw Bram and Alan together, he knew his friend would be okay. Alan was a sweet man, steady and calm. He also had the temperament from his days playing baseball to keep up with Bram. Theirs was the kind of love he wanted for himself.

If his version of someone like Alan existed.

Josef fiddled with the nub of rubber on the edge of the tablet that had torn loose. "My coach asked me to get my head in the game for this weekend. He doesn't know about my past, but he knows enough to figure out I've got a lot on my mind. I don't want to let the boys down, but I can't figure this out."

"Have you talked to Mark?" Bram asked. "Or is it something else?"

"When I see the boys, I remember being in their position and wanting so much to impress my father. Then the old bastard called me names because I'm gay. Said I wasn't a man or a decent player because of my sexuality. I'm, on one hand, in awe of the boys and on the other, frustrated that they're sailing when I hit choppy waters."

"You had more than choppy waters. You sailed through a goddamn hurricane," Dante said. "It wasn't fair and I wish you'd have let me say something back then. I knew you were hurting."

He knew. Dante had been his first champion and crush—not that he'd tell Dante he'd been interested in him. That's all he needed—to inflate Dante's ego more than it already was, or encourage him too much.

"I did." Josef sighed and massaged his forehead. "The worst part is that I want to see the boys succeed, but I'm secretly angry with them for not having to navigate what I did. I wish I could go back to my younger self and speak up for myself, but I can't change the past and my father's dead. Can't talk to a ghost."

"No, but has Mark given you some ideas? Maybe write a letter or two or ten to him and burn them?" Bram asked. "We have students do that sometimes."

"Make a video or even just an audio recording where you get it all out, then delete it?" Tim asked.

"Gone to the cemetery and said what needed to be said?" Dante asked. "I'll come out and run interference in case someone questions you."

He appreciated their ideas.

"Maybe a journal." Bram shrugged. "Write it all down over the course of days or weeks or whatever, then either lock it up or shred it?"

"I like the fire idea," Tim said. "It's so destructive."

"You would," Josef replied. Dante drove him crazy, but he rather liked his idea. "I know this sounds silly. I'm forty-six years old and tired as hell of this whole thing. It's a weight around my neck."

"Then let's get rid of it." Dante applauded. "You've got this."

"You sound like a coach." He crooked his brow, but the ideas churned through his head. He sent Dante a private text chat.

Would you be willing to come to town Sunday? Accompany me to the cemetery?

The three dots flickered as Dante read and typed a reply. His heart pounded as he waited to see what Dante might say. Part of him knew Dante would agree, but a piece of him worried his friend would turn him down due to a scheduling conflict.

A moment later, the reply came.

What time? Where are we meeting? Your place?

Ah, he could rely on his oldest friend. He barely paid attention to the cross chatter, despite the fact it was about him.

Noon?

He turned his attention back to the main chat. "Sorry."

"We know you're not paying attention. We just offered to sell your football memorabilia," Tim said. "For a buck."

"Asshole." But he loved his friends. They kept him in line.

Dante's reply came before the small box darkened.

Done. See you then.

Good. He could work with that.

"So you're going to talk to Dante, you're going to let go of some of this anger and coach the hell out of the game on Saturday? Then hunt for a boyfriend?" Tim asked. "You'll give yourself a chance?"

"Yes." He nodded and made a snap decision. "I'm going to try a dating site." It was foolhardy and could be another dead end. But he had to try.

"You were thinking about it?" Bram asked. "Are you permitted? It's not in your coaching contract to keep from doing that kind of thing? It might not be. Our teachers aren't supposed to, but that's because it's all searchable."

"It's not." He wasn't sure, but he'd look. He hadn't signed up yet, so it wasn't too late.

"Good. Just keep your profile more or less clean," Bram said. "Learn from past mistakes we've all made."

"I know." He would. He needed a change. Needed to find someone for himself. The bar scene wasn't happening—people wanted to talk sports and while he wanted someone who understood football, he didn't want an armchair quarterback. "I'm not doing the dating coach thing, either. I don't want to be alone, but the only wingmen I want are you all."

Tim bowed. "Always."

Bram grinned. "I didn't use the dating coach method, so I can't say it's good or bad, but I get it. You need who you trust."

"I do," Josef said. "I'm tired of being alone."

"I get it," Dante said. "It's not fun going to parties on your own. People get this idea they need to push you to someone. Gotta be the matchmaker. What if you don't want that? What if you're not interested in the guy's friend's cousin's brother? What if you're just there to listen to the band? You just want to hear good music, take five minutes from your life and forget you're a parent who feels like his son isn't listening to him?" His eyes widened and he stopped talking.

"You just outed yourself and let us know what's finally bothering you, too," Tim said. "Dante, you're not invincible."

"We're here to help Josef. I'm not important." Dante closed his window, leaving that part of the screen dark.

"Well." Bram crooked his brow and shook his head. "We cut a little too close to the bone. You need to do what you need to do, Jos. If it's a profile, then cool. If it's something else, just as cool. Be smart, but follow…" He rolled his eyes.

"His heart?" Tim asked. "You've been at the school for too long, talking in motivational poster lingo."

"I am," Bram said. "Keep us posted and don't be a stranger. We do care about you."

"Ditto," Tim said. "We're trying to help."

"I know, and I appreciate it." Even if they were somewhat pushy about it. "I'm going to the cemetery and say my piece to Dad — even if he can't hear me."

"Good." Bram sat up straighter. "Gotta go. Next meeting starts in five minutes."

"If he's going, then I guess I am, too." Tim waved before darkening his screen.

Bram darkened his at the same time, leaving Josef alone.

Although he wasn't in the chat any longer, he wasn't lonely. They'd given him the help he'd needed and a direction. Things weren't going exactly as he wanted, but they would be soon enough. Once he let go some of his baggage and forgave himself, he'd be able to move forward.

Not long now.